LOUISA MAY ALCOTT was born in Germantown, Pennsylvania, in 1832, the second of four daughters of Abba May
Alcott and Bronson Alcott, the prominent transcendentalist
thinker and social reformer. Raised in Concord, Massachusetts, and educated by her father, Alcott early on came under
the influence of the great men of his circle: Emerson, Hawthorne, the preacher Theodore Parker, and Thoreau. From
her youth, she worked at various tasks to help support her
family: sewing, teaching, domestic service, and writing. In
1862, she volunteered to serve as an army nurse in a Union
hospital during the Civil War—an experience that provided
her with material for her first successful book, *Hospital
Sketches* (1863). Between 1863 and 1869, she published
anonymous and pseudonymous Gothic romances and lurid
thrillers. But fame came with the publication of her *Little
Women* (1868–69), a novel based on the childhood adven-
tures of the four Alcott sisters, which received immense
popular acclaim and brought her financial security as well as
the conviction to continue in her career as a writer. In the
wake of *Little Women*'s popularity, she brought out *An Old-
Fashioned Girl* (1870), *Little Men* (1871), *Eight Cousins* (1875),
Rose in Bloom (1876), *Jo's Boys* (1886), and other books for
children, as well as two adult novels, *Moods* (1865) and *Work*
(1873). An active participant in the woman's suffrage and
temperance movements during the last decade of her life,
Alcott died in Boston in 1888, on the day her father was
buried.

Joel Myerson, Carolina Distinguished Professor of American Literature at the University of South Carolina, has edited *Studies in the American Renaissance* (1977–1996) and published more than thirty books on transcendentalism and related topics.

Daniel Shealy, Professor of English at the University of North Carolina-Charlotte, has published numerous articles on Louisa May Alcott.

Together, Myerson and Shealy have co-edited five books on Alcott, including *The Selected Letters of Louisa May Alcott* and *The Journals of Louisa May Alcott*.

THE
INHERITANCE

LOUISA MAY ALCOTT

EDITED WITH

AN INTRODUCTION AND NOTES BY

JOEL MYERSON AND DANIEL SHEALY

PENGUIN BOOKS

PENGUIN BOOKS
Published by the Penguin Group
Penguin Group (USA) Inc., 375 Hudson Street, New York, New York 10014, U.S.A.
Penguin Books Ltd, 80 Strand, London WC2R 0RL, England
Penguin Books Australia Ltd, 250 Camberwell Road, Camberwell, Victoria 3124, Australia
Penguin Books Canada Ltd, 10 Alcorn Avenue, Toronto, Ontario, Canada M4V 3B2
Penguin Books India (P) Ltd, 11 Community Centre, Panchsheel Park, New Delhi – 110 017, India
Penguin Books (N.Z.) Ltd, Cnr Rosedale and Airborne Roads, Albany, Auckland, New Zealand
Penguin Books (South Africa) (Pty) Ltd, 24 Sturdee Avenue,
Rosebank, Johannesburg 2196, South Africa

Penguin Books Ltd, Registered Offices: 80 Strand, London WC2R 0RL, England

First published in the United States of America by
Dutton Children's Books, a division of Penguin Books USA Inc. 1997
This edition with an introduction and notes by Joel Myerson
and Daniel Shealy published in Penguin Books 1998

9   10   8

Copyright © Charles Pratt, Frederick Pratt, and John Pratt, 1997
Introduction, notes, and afterword copyright © Joel Myerson
and Daniel Shealy, 1997, 1998
All rights reserved

LIBRARY OF CONGRESS CATALOGING IN PUBLICATION DATA
Alcott, Louisa May, 1832–1888.
The inheritance / Louisa May Alcott; edited with an introduction
and notes by Joel Myerson and Daniel Shealy.
p.   cm.—(Penguin classics)
Includes bibliographical references.
ISBN 0 14 04.3666 9
1. Orphans—England—Fiction.   2. England—Fiction.   I. Myerson,
Joel.   II. Shealy, Daniel.   III. Title.   IV. Series.
PS1017.I54   1998
813'.4—dc21   97–26241

Printed in the United States of America
Set in Bembo
Designed by Alice Sorensen

CONTENTS

INTRODUCTION

In *Little Women,* Jo March confidently reveals to Laurie her dream of building a castle in the air: "I'd have a stable full of Arabian steeds, rooms piled with books, and I'd write out of a magic inkstand, so that my works should be . . . famous. I want to do something splendid before I go into my castle—something heroic or wonderful that won't be forgotten after I'm dead. I don't know what, but I'm on the watch for it and mean to astonish you all someday. I think I shall write books and get rich and famous."[1] Alcott indeed fulfilled this dream, becoming one of the best-selling authors of the nineteenth century. At her death, she had written twenty-eight books, both novels and collections of tales, and published more than three hundred stories and articles in periodicals. It is estimated that she earned approximately $103,375 on her book publications alone during the period 1868 to 1886, not including royalties from European sales.[2] By comparison, Henry James's royalities from book sales, both in America and abroad, amounted to $58,503 during the same eighteen-year period.[3] Herman Melville, on the other hand, earned only $10,444.33 from all book sales during his lifetime.[4] However, Alcott's rise to fame was hardly meteoric. She had learned and mastered her craft at a young age and quickly developed the ability to gauge the public marketplace, but it took her almost twenty years to achieve her first big success, *Little Women*.

The Inheritance was one of her earliest steps along the road to literary fame. According to Alcott's comments on the manuscript, *The Inheritance* was written in 1849, when she was seventeen years old. It predates her first published piece, a poem, by several years and her first published novel by fifteen years. Written in Boston, possibly while the family lived at High Street, the work must have held an important place in the author's heart, since she never destroyed it. Was the book written with an eye toward publication or only for the love of creation, as an exercise of the imagination? Unfortunately, readers may never know. No clues as to the book's origins exist. None of Alcott's extant letters or journals or the private writings of her family and friends provide any details of the novel's composition.

Upon the birth of Louisa May Alcott on November 29, 1832, her father, Amos Bronson Alcott, wrote Colonel Joseph May, his father-in-law, to announce the arrival of his second child. He expressed the wish that his newborn girl would "eventually deserve a place in the estimation of society."[5] That desire would not be so easily won. Alcott's life would be a pilgrim's progress, filled with its Vanity Fairs and Sloughs of Despond. Life for "the pathetic family," as Louisa often called the Alcotts, would be one of disappointment, tragedy, loss, and near poverty, especially during her childhood and teenage years.[6] But it was also one of creativity and intellectual stimulation.

When Bronson Alcott and Abigail May were married at King's Chapel, Boston, many present at the wedding must have puzzled over the union. The two young people possessed such different backgrounds. Alcott, born on November 29, 1799, was the son of poor Connecticut farmers. By the age of eighteen, he was already a peddler, selling his wares in the South. But making his living as a traveling merchant was not to be his calling. Instead, he was drawn to books, to the life of the mind, and to teaching. His first teaching job brought him home to Connecticut, where he eventually met the Reverend Samuel Joseph May and his sister Abigail May in 1827. While Alcott had experienced the hard life of farming, the uncertainty of success as a peddler, and the meager salary of a schoolteacher, Abigail May's life was just the opposite. Born in 1800, in Boston, she was the youngest of the twelve children of Colonel Joseph May, a wealthy shipbuilder and one of the city's distinguished citizens. Among her ancestors were the Puritan minister Samuel Sewall, most remembered for his role at the infamous Salem witchcraft trials of 1692, and John Hancock, one of the leaders of the American Revolution.

At a time when education for women was not highly valued, Abigail was educated at home by a tutor and shared the May family characteristic of helping the poor and needy. However, when Bronson proposed in 1828, she decided not to marry him until his future was more certain. With the May family's influence, Bronson was able to secure a teaching position at Boston's Infant School, and the two were finally married in 1830. Less than a year later, their first daughter, Anna, was born. Louisa May Alcott followed in 1832.

Supported financially by the Philadelphia Quakers, Bronson opened an academy in Germantown, Pennsylvania, but in 1834 the aid ended, and the family returned to Boston with little money and two young girls. By September 1834, Alcott was able to open Temple School, assisted by Elizabeth Palmer Peabody. It was his opportunity to put his educational philosophy into practice. His 1830 pamphlet *Observations on the Principles of Infant Instruction* forthrightly states, "Infant education when adapted to the human being, is founded on the great principle, that every infant is already in possession of the faculties and apparatus required for his instruction, and, that by a law of his constitution, he uses these to a great extent himself; that the office of instruction is chiefly to facilitate this process, and to accompany the child in his progress rather than to drive or even to lead him."[7]

Alcott's methods at his Temple School demonstrated this radical educational philosophy. Contrary to the reliance on rote education at the time, Alcott attemped to make his charges aware of the divinity within themselves by turning their attention inward so that, having discovered their inner power, they might use it in guiding their outward lives. Education to Alcott was a joy and not an enforced labor. He believed in the positive influence of the home, and in his schoolroom he attempted to re-create a homelike atmosphere. In part because of this, his classroom was distinguished by open spaces and pleasant surroundings, with art objects and books prominently displayed. His method was inductive and Socratic: By questioning his students he let them discover answers instead of merely telling them rules. Books were supplemental to these discussions; Alcott deplored schools where learning consisted solely of memorizing texts. There was no corporal punishment at Alcott's school; problem children were merely excluded from the group until they demonstrated a desire to return by settling down.

Bronson's educational principles are clearly reflected in his daughter Louisa's works. In *Little Women* and its sequels, Jo March's desire to be a teacher is obviously patterned on her father's chosen profession, and the Plumfield School is an updated version of Bronson's Temple School. The Socratic method practiced by her father finds its way into Marmee's practice of letting the girls discover life for themselves: "Mrs. March knew that experience was an excellent teacher, and when it was possible she left her children to learn alone the lessons which she would gladly have made easier, if they had not objected to taking advice as much as they did salts and senna."[8]

Bronson's educational philosophy was innovative, and for almost two years the Temple School was successful, but when Bronson published *Conversations with Children on the Gospels*, a work that explained his teaching methods, the more conservative Bostonians began to brand the teacher as a radical. Parents withdrew their children, and when Alcott admitted a young black girl in 1839, almost all support was lost and the enterprise closed.

The "pathetic family," which now included a third daughter, Elizabeth, born in 1835, moved to Concord, Massachusetts, where Bronson could be near his friend Ralph Waldo Emerson, whom he had met in the mid-1830s. Bronson gave up his teaching and focused on writing—without any literary or financial success. As the family struggled to survive, a fourth daughter, Abby May, was born in July 1840 in Concord. After a trip to England during 1841 and 1842, a voyage underwritten primarily by Emerson, Alcott returned with a British friend and fellow reformer, Charles Lane. Together, the two planned to establish a new Eden in America.

On approximately one hundred acres outside of rural Harvard, Massachusetts, the two men located their utopian experiment, earnestly named Fruitlands. Arriving at the chosen site on June 1, 1843, they were filled with the promise of a communal life. Committed to a vegetarian diet, they set about planting vegetables and fruit. However, the men soon spent more time spreading their philosophy and attracting new members than they did producing crops. Most of the work fell upon the women, especially Abigail Alcott and her daughters. Emerson, who paid them a visit in July 1843, wisely recorded in his journal, "They look well in July. We will see them in December."[9] By the end of 1843, the entire experiment had collapsed. The autumn harvest was meager, and fuel for the coming winter was not in place. Young Louisa noted sadly in her journal, "I was very unhappy. Anna and I cried in bed, and I prayed God to keep us all together."[10] By January 1844, the Alcotts sought refuge a few miles away in Still River, Massachusetts. In the fall of that year, they returned to Concord.

With the inheritance gained from the death of Abigail's father and an additional sum supplied by Emerson, the Alcotts purchased a home on Lexington Road, a short distance from Emerson's own dwelling. Living at Hillside, as Bronson called the new home, would prove a happy time for young Louisa, although her father was still unable to secure a teaching position. The teenage Louisa found herself surrounded by her father's friends, men and women who were among the creators of an emerging American literature—Ralph Waldo Emerson, Henry David Thoreau, Margaret Fuller, and Nathaniel Hawthorne. Louisa claimed that the "Concord days were the happiest of my life, for we had charming playmates in the little Emersons, [Ellery] Channings, Hawthornes, . . . with the illustrious parents and their friends to enjoy our pranks and share our excursions."[11]

During this period in Concord, Alcott herself became friends with Thoreau and Emerson, two individuals who would greatly influence her life. She and her family often visited Thoreau at his cabin on Walden Pond, where he would row the children along the shoreline in his boat or saunter with them through the Concord woods on huckleberrying parties. He would also relate marvelous tales of nature's woodland fairies to the enchanted young girls. Thoreau, in turn, would visit the Alcotts at Hillside, sitting for hours in the parlor conversing with Bronson. Emerson also held a special place in Louisa's heart. He was, she once claimed, her "beloved 'Master.' "[12] She would, at her whim, venture into Emerson's study in search of new books to read and new worlds to explore. As she listened carefully, he would suggest suitable choices. When he offered her *Goethe's Correspondence with a Child,* the letters between Bettine von Arnim and Johann Wolfgang von Goethe that showed a strong pupil–master relationship, Alcott was "at once fired with the desire to be a second Bettine, making my father's friend my Goethe." She confessed to writing many letters to him, "but was wise enough never to send them." Instead, she "left wild flowers on the doorstep . . . , sung Mignon's song in very bad German under his window, and was fond of wandering by moonlight, or sitting in a cherry-tree at midnight till the owls scared me to bed."[13] Both Emerson's and Thoreau's ideas of self-reliance and reform would influence Louisa's life and fiction. Not only would she take an active role in the anti-slavery movement and the women's rights movement, but she would incorporate ideas for the improvement of the individual and society in her fiction, such as *Little Men* (1871) and *Rose in Bloom* (1876). What else would one expect from the woman who once signed her letters, "Yours for reforms of all kinds."[14]

Literature was always a part of Alcott's life. Reading was an escape from the everyday troubles of her family's struggles, and it is no surprise that she loved sentimental tales of romance and faraway places. As a young girl, Louisa was educated primarily by her father, and she enjoyed a variety of books. *Pilgrim's Progress,* which would later inspire the structure of *Little Women*, was a family favorite, a volume that her father would read each year. As early as 1843, she read *Oliver Twist*, and Charles Dickens would remain one of her favorite authors throughout her life. Maria Edgeworth's *Rosamond*, a colleciton of tales for children, was another early favorite. She delighted in Charlotte Brontë's Gothic-influenced *Jane Eyre* and in Sir Walter Scott's heroic tales of knighthood, especially his novel *Kenilworth* (one of three novels whose characters would later appear in *The Inheritance*).

Alcott and her sisters would also bring to life the stories from the books they read. In the mid-1840s, the Alcott girls adapted various works, such as ones by Dickens, into plays, which they performed for family and friends. Louisa and her older sister, Anna, also wrote their own dramas, and the Hillside barn was transformed into a theater as the girls strutted the boards. When she was seventeen, the same age she wrote *The Inheritance*, Louisa confessed in her journal how she hoped to achieve success: "Anna wants to be an actress, and so do I. We could make plenty of money perhaps, and it is a very gay life. Mother says we are too young and must wait. . . . I like tragic plays. . . . We get up fine ones, and make harps, castles, armor, dresses, waterfalls, and thunder, and have great fun."[15] These childhood plays found their way into *Little Women*, where in the second chapter the young March girls enact "The Witch's Curse, an Operatic Tragedy" as Christmas entertainment. Much later in life, Anna Alcott published a collection of these childhood plays, titled *Comic Tragedies Written by "Jo" and "Meg" and Acted by the "Little Women"* (1893), which included "Norna; or, The Witch's Curse," an obvious forerunner to the play enacted in *Little Women*. Anna noted that after a day of work, the "greatest delight of the girls was to transform themselves into queens, knights, and cavaliers of high degree, and ascend into a world of fancy and romance."[16] Louisa herself later recollected that in one play, she "took five parts and Anna four, with lightning changes of costume, and characters varying from a Greek prince in silver armor to a murderer in chains."[17]

But the idyll in Concord soon ended. As Louisa wrote, Bronson "went away to hold his classes and conversations, and we women folk began to feel that we also might do something. So one gloomy November day we decided to move to Boston and try our fate again after some years in the wilderness."[18] While Louisa and Anna taught school, Abigail began to help the poor, especially the Irish immigrants, and Bronson continued his conversations with little prospect of money. Louisa's desire to write also grew in the bustling city, and she began to practice at home. A family newspaper, *The Olive Leaf*, was first composed in July 1849, later to be followed by *The Pickwick Portfolio*. In this family production, all four sisters contributed poetry, notices, or stories, but Louisa's efforts were most notable.

Alcott's early attempts at writing were influenced by the melodrama of the theater and the sentimental and Gothic literature that was popular at the time. Foreign life was exotic to her; lords and ladies, castles, and counts were far removed from the toil of everyday life in Boston, where the family struggled to get by. As Anna once claimed: "Of the world they [the Alcott sisters] knew nothing; lovers were ideal beings, clothed with all the beauty of their innocent imaginations. Love was a blissful dream; constancy, truth, courage, and virtue quite every-day affairs of life. Their few novels furnished the romantic element; the favorite fairy-tales gave them material for the supernatural; and their stong dramatic taste enabled them to infuse both fire and pathos into absurd situations."[19]

Other than manuscript copies of the sisters' family newspapers, the only evidence of Louisa's literary efforts during this time is the manuscript of *The Inheritance*. Alcott, in a note at the front of the manuscript, indicated that she wrote the book at age seventeen at High Street, Boston.[20] However, she had recently turned eighteen when the family moved to 50 High Street in December 1850. Alcott, later in her life, most noticeably upon her mother's death in 1877, reviewed her writings, often making marginal comments. The handwriting reveals that the note about the composition of the novel was added at a much later date. Since the family moved several times during their stay in Boston (1848 to 1850), it is most likely that Alcott, by the time she attached the note, had forgotten the exact location where she had written the book. Wherever the location of its composition, the book remains, without question, her first sustained piece of fiction, her first novel.

The Inheritance provides readers with the starting point of a remarkable career. In the novel, Alcott focuses on the relationship among three girls, as she does similarly in *Little Women* with the four sisters. She even names one of her major characters Amy, a name she would later reclaim for the artistic March sister. As in her later fiction, the traits of honesty, trust, and family fidelity are championed. She even nods to her love of the theater by creating a tableau scene where the characters pose as famous historical or fictional figures. Set at Lord Hamilton's English manor, the book tells the story of Edith Adelon, an Italian orphan who had been brought home by the now deceased Lord Hamilton to serve as a playmate for his daughter, Amy. Edith's "beauty, gentleness and lovely voice" had won the lord's affections, and she soon became friend and companion to Amy and her brother, Lord Arthur.[21] As she grew into womanhood, Edith became "beautiful and richly gifted," qualities that disturb the jealous and vengeful Lady Ida Clare, the niece of Lady Hamilton. Lady Ida, whose "proud heart longed for rank and wealth," views the Italian girl as competition for "every word of courtesy or kindness given"; when noble Lord Percy arrives at the manor, Lady Ida despises the looks of admiration he bestows upon Edith. No longer content to sit idly by, she plots to drive the girl away. Using the fictional devices of the Gothic romance, Alcott hinges Edith's rescue on a long-hidden secret.

Alcott's *The Inheritance* is not unlike most of the popular fiction of its era. Indeed, sentimental novels ruled the literary marketplace in America during the first half of the nineteenth century. As the critic Herbert Ross Brown points out, "The didactic-sentimental tale of domestic manners proved to be so congenial to female taste and talent that more than one third of the American novels published before the advent of [James Fenimore] Cooper's *Precaution* in 1820 were written by women."[22] By midcentury, Hawthorne himself would complain to his publisher about the "mob of scribbling women" who dominated the list of best-selling books.[23] The sentimental novel, or novel of sensibility, began in England with the publication of Samuel Richardson's *Pamela; or, Virtue Rewarded* in 1740. Other major authors of the period soon followed; Henry

Fielding's *Tom Jones* (1749), Tobias Smollett's *Roderick Random* (1748), Laurence Stern's *Tristam Shandy* (1760–67), and Jane Austen's *Sense and Sensibility* (1811) are all examples of the sentimental novel. Charles Dickens's *The Old Curiosity Shop* (1841) worked the same literary vein. Of course, lesser authors also copied the style as the growing reading public began to clamor for more novels. America, looking to England for its literary influences, soon imitated the popular genre. The first novel published in America, William Hill Brown's *The Power of Sympathy; or, The Triumph of Nature* (1789), was a sentimental tale, and it was soon followed by America's first best-seller, *Charlotte: A Tale of Truth* (1791), written by Susanna Haswell Rowson. The sentimental novel, especially that of the late eighteenth century, "emphasized the tearful distresses of the virtuous, either at their own sorrows or at those of their friends; some of them represented in addition a sensitivity to beauty or sublimity."[24]

At the same time that the sentimental novel was born, another genre, the Gothic romance, appeared. In 1764, the English author Horace Walpole published *The Castle of Otranto: A Gothic Story*. With its medieval setting, Walpole's book served as the model for other novels, such as Ann Radcliffe's *The Mysteries of Udolpho* (1794) and Matthew Gregory Lewis's *The Monk* (1796). Later British works, such as Emily Brontë's *Wuthering Heights* (1847), Charlotte Brontë's *Jane Eyre* (1847), and Charles Dickens's *Great Expectations* (1860), also contained Gothic elements.

The Gothic novel revealed the world of nightmares and horror with its crumbling castles, stormy nights, innocent heroines, secret panels, and supernatural events. In America, Charles Brockdon Brown's *Wieland; or, The Transformation* (1798) was influenced by the British Gothic romance. The short stories Edgar Allan Poe wrote during the 1830s and 1840s certainly contained Gothic strains, as did Nathaniel Hawthorne's *The House of the Seven Gables* (1852) with its secret passageway and family curse.

While it is by no means clear that Alcott read this long list of works, she certainly had read Charlotte Brontë, Dickens, and Hawthorne. She was well read in the British classics as well, as was her father, and she delighted in the popular fiction of her day. Alcott had more than a passing familiarity with both the sentimental novel and the Gothic romance, and both genres influenced *The Inheritance*. Set at Hamilton Manor, "an old, decaying castle" with "gray old" towers and arches covered with ivy, the book captures the atmosphere of the Gothic romance, complete with "the haunted ruins" of an "ancient chapel." But the setting also evokes what Brown calls the landscape of the sentimental novel: "When the sentimental heroine ventured out of doors there was rung down upon the stage a backdrop drenched in pale moonlight and painted in the ultra-romantic style."[25] In fact, Alcott first introduces Edith in a scene where she is bathed in the "soft light" of the moon as she plays the organ and sings alone in the old chapel. Later, as the Hamiltons hold a celebration for the villagers,

Lord Percy and Edith glide in a boat on the moonlit lake. As Edith sings, Percy falls more in love and confesses to Edith, "How can I feel weariness with moonlight such as this and music like your own? If the voyage of life were half as pleasant, few would wish it ended." Even the treacherous crags that Edith loves so well bring to mind the wild landscapes, such as the heaths and moors, so loved by the sentimentalist writer.

Not only the landscape of *The Inheritance* fits the sentimental formula but also the markedly flat characters that populate it. One-dimensional characters allowed the reader to easily see good and evil without any ambiguity. Lord Percy whose "true heart within shines clearly out and gives a quiet beauty to his face," falls in love with Edith, who possesses the outward appearance of "an angel's calm and almost holy beauty" and the inward quality of "as pure a heart—gentle, true, and tender." Both major characters, like the typical sentimental hero or heroine, are ministers of charity. Brown states that the "humanitarian impulse" was a mainstay of the sentimental character: "No belief was more highly cherished and more eloquently proclaimed than that of the inherent nobility of the human heart." The sentimentalist, he argues, "exalted pity as one of the major virtues" and believed firmly in "the perfectibility of man."[26] Edith is praised for her "faithful care and silent deeds of charity," whether it is helping the dying old servant Theresa or maternally watching over the woman's young son, Louis. As Brown notes, "The domestic scene provided a more convenient sphere for philanthropic activity than foreign courts."[27] As a match for Edith's kindness, Lord Percy gives little regard to his riches; instead, he "prized far more the purity and worth of noble hearts. . . . Forgetful of the title that he bore, he went among the suffering and the poor and won from them their gratitude and love." These two angels of mercy would appear many times in Alcott's reform-minded fiction, most notably in *Little Women* as Beth, who functions as that novel's "angel in the house," even sacrificing her life after caring for the poor Hummel baby who has contracted scarlet fever.

Like many well-known characters in the sentimental novel, Edith is an orphan: "Her mother had died and her father was unknown." Lord Hamilton, who discovered the ten-year-old Edith "singing in the garden," was "touched by her lonely, friendless situation . . . so he brought the homeless child to England." All she remembered of her "childhood is that, with my mother, I dwelt in a poor and humble home with few joys but her love and no friends but a kind old peasant." With few remembrances of her mother and no knowledge of her father, Edith is without family, without a past, even though the Hamiltons treat her as one of their own. As an orphan, she is an outsider, one who often is isolated from the family. She even loves "to be alone and wander in the woods, as most romantic governesses do." Being an orphan also makes Edith a more vulnerable character, like many of her sentimental orphan counterparts, such as Jane Eyre, Tom Jones, and Oliver Twist.

Her vulnerability makes her an easy prey for the novel's evil characters, Lady Ida Clare and Lord Arlington. Ida, who fears Edith will destroy her chances of romance with the wealthy Lord Percy, readily confesses her dislike of the Italian servant: "You are young and lovely, and in spite of poverty and humble birth, you win respect and admiration from those above you. You have no right to stand between me and my happiness as you do, and I hate you for it." As an outsider in the family, Edith refuses to confront the Hamiltons about the mistreatment she receives at the hands and tongue of their relative.

While she receives harsh words from Lady Ida, Edith is even more vulnerable to the cruel Lord Arlington: "Young, thoughtless, and gay, he had been spoiled by the world. Now, selfish, passionate, discontented, and tired of the pleasures he had once enjoyed, he was more easily charmed by Edith's pure and gentle nature, for it was new. Therefore, he pursued this pleasing novelty as he did all things, careless of the pain he gave and bent on gaining what he sought. From the hour when he stood looking on as she knelt among the flowers with the rose evening light upon her pure, pale face, she was ever before him, and he longed to win her more and more." Arlington's intentions form the novel's seduction motif, a standard device of the sentimental novel. Beginning with Richardson's *Pamela*, the theme of the young, innocent woman being pursued by the evil seducer who is intent on capturing his prey and forcing her to succumb to his passion became a popular mainstay of the sentimental novel both in Britain and America. Even America's two earliest novels, *The Power of Sympathy* and *Charlotte: A Tale of Truth*, stressed the corruption of the seducer.

While Alcott tones down the language employed by the early sentimentalists, she clearly shows how Arlington uses his domineering force to place Edith in awkward situations. On the horseback ride with Arthur, Amy, and Ida, Arlington first confronts Edith about his desire, but she steadfastly refuses his love: "With blushing dignity, in few but simple words she thanked him for the honor. . . . When he placed himself before her, passionately vowing he should remain till she had given another and a kinder answer, she repeated her refusal. Freeing her hand from his rude grasp, she touched her horse and, with a silent look of calm contempt, passed by . . . with the bright flush on her cheek and the indignant light still in her eye." But Arlington is not so easily deterred: "And now Edith had another trial to grieve and worry her, for Lord Arlington, to vent his anger and his disappointed passion, seemed to delight in doing all that lay in his power to make her feel the jealous love he still cherished for her."

Lord Arlington's steady attempt to seduce Edith reaches its climax in the forest, a setting filled with sexual connotations. Standing before her in the shaded pathway, Arlington beseeches her once again: "Think well before you cast away what few would offer one so poor and friendless as yourself. Your grace and beauty captivate me, and I forget all else in the joy of winning you." Again, Edith denies him: "Poor and humble as I am, your wealth can never buy my love, nor your rank command respect for one who has rendered me unhappy by a selfish passion that cannot feel respect for my unfriended state, nor shame for the sorrow it has caused me. . . . Let me pass. I will not be detained." Lord Arlington, whose "dark cheek burned at Edith's calm rebuke," angrily approaches Edith, declaring, "Nay, never look so proudly. You shall learn to fear me if you will not love." Alcott then writes, "With flashing eyes and lips white with passion, he watched her cheek grow pale with terror as she leaned trembling against a tree." A possible rape is suddenly thwarted by Lord Percy's appearance, and the seducer soon departs Hamilton Manor. The burdens that Edith bears only make her more honorable in the reader's eyes. As Lord Percy observes: "Amid the trials she so silently was bearing still grew the gratitude and love she bore to those around her and still lay the deep, longing wish for tenderness and true affection, which none ever guessed and none ever sought to give."

With Edith's desire for true love and her ability to withstand the advances of Arlington and the jealousy of Ida, she serves as a fitting sentimental heroine who well deserves an inheritance. Alcott, of course, early in the novel, makes it known that Edith is no ordinary orphan when Arthur

Hamilton declares, "Edith is of a good, perhaps a noble family, for there is a dignity and highborn look about her that would become any lady in the land." Thus, the sudden turn of fortune, as Edith is discovered to be the cousin of Arthur and Amy and the rightful heir to the Hamilton estate and fortune, is not so great an overturning of the ordered world. Neither was the dramatic use of a hidden legacy unheard of in the literature of the period. Howard W. Fulweiler points out in his study of the sentimental novel that the "issue of inheritance plays an important role in the nineteenth-century generally."[28] He argues that such works as Jane Austen's *Pride and Prejudice* (1813), among others, revolve around a plot device of inheritance and property. While Edith does inherit great wealth, she refuses to accept it, tearing up the newly discovered will and declaring, "Now I am the poor orphan girl again." What she most desires is love of family, not riches, and she implores Lady Hamilton: "In return for this act, let me call you mother and be a faithful, loving child, for you can never know how sad it is to be so young and yet so utterly alone." Edith also wins the love of Lord Percy; she, like Jane Eyre, does not find a father, but a lover. In her first novel, Alcott begins the examination of a theme that would continue throughout her career. For Alcott, as for Edith Adelon, family is the most noble inheritance. As Jo March declares, more than twenty years later, "I do think that families are the most beautiful things in all the world!"[29]

As *The Inheritance* proves, Alcott drew upon the fiction

of her time for her early literary efforts. Her first published work was "Sunlight," a poem that appeared under the pseudonym Flora Fairfield in *Peterson's Magazine* in September 1851, when she was almost nineteen years old. Less than a year later, in May 1852, her first published story appeared in the *Olive Branch*, a magazine of polite literature. "The Rival Painters: A Tale of Rome" revolves around two painters, Guido and Count Ferdinand, who are enthralled with the beautiful Madeline, the daughter of an old artist. Ferdinand had "wealth, rank, a splendid home, and a heart full of love" for Madeline, while Guido possessed only "a noble soul and a rare talent for painting." Madeline's father, unable to select the better husband, promises his daughter to the one who "painted a picture the most perfect in grace, and beauty of form, design and coloring." The wealthy count paints Madeline; however, the young Guido chooses his own mother as his subject. The old artist is so impressed that he gives his daughter's hand to the poor Guido, saying, "I ask no greater wealth for my child than the love of so noble a son."[30] Alcott was paid five dollars for her story; however, she was more impressed that her own writing was in print. The dream of becoming an author was getting closer. The tale, Alcott reveals in her journal, "was written in Concord when I was sixteen. . . . Read it aloud to sisters, and when they praised it, not knowing the author, I proudly announced her name."[31] Alcott later used this exact scene in *Little*

Women when Jo reads "The Rival Painters" aloud to her sisters, who do not know the author.

Her second story, "The Masked Marrriage," would soon follow in December 1852. This story, also set in Italy, recounts a tale of true love that must overcome a greedy parent. Ferdinand de Vere, an Englishman, falls in love with Alice de Adelon, daughter of Count de Adelon. However, the count wants his daughter to marry the wealthy Italian Count Antonio. By accident, Ferdinand discovers an old woman who reveals a long-hidden secret that will allow him to marry Alice. Once engaged to Ferdinand's father, the old woman was rejected in favor of a rich lady. Furious at Ferdinand's father, the woman stole his will; thus, the family fortune, upon his death, went to another kinsman—Count Antonio. Wanting to right her wrong before her death, the old woman returns the will to Ferdinand, restoring him as the rightful heir. Learning this news, Count Antonio leaves the country. However, the wedding goes on as planned since Alice de Adelon's father is not aware of the turn of events. To everyone's dismay, when the groom enters the church, he is masked. Only when the vows are complete does Ferdinand remove his disguise and reveal to his greedy father-in-law that he has inherited great wealth. Of course, this tale in some ways resembles *The Inheritance*. Alice de Adelon and Edith Adelon not only share a surname, but both are from Italy. The two narratives, set among the castles of royalty, revolve around a hidden legacy. Clearly, the author went back to her unpublished novel for inspiration.

Poems and stories continued to pour from Alcott's pen, and in December 1854, her first book, *Flower Fables*, was published. A collection of didactic tales set in a peaceful fairy kingdom, these stories were originally told to Ellen Emerson, the younger daughter of Ralph Waldo Emerson. Inspired by the woodland fairy tales once related to Alcott by Thoreau, *Flower Fables* received a favorable review in *The Saturday Evening Gazette*, a periodical to which Alcott was already contributing short stories: "Very sweet are these legends of faery land, which those of our friends, who are so fond of tales of enchantment, will, we are sure, peruse with avidity."[32] When the book was published, Alcott presented her mother a copy, along with a note telling her that into "your Christmas stocking I have put my 'first born,' knowing that you will accept it with all its faults (for grandmothers are always kind), and look upon it merely as an earnest of what I may yet do; for, with so much to cheer me on, I hope to pass in time from fairies and fables to men and realities."[33]

As the 1850s progressed, "realities" would soon intrude. In September 1857, the Alcott family returned to Concord, purchasing a home next door to their former residence. Bronson christened the new domicile Orchard House; Louisa less romantically called it "Apple Slump."[34] Again Bronson was surrounded by the comfort of his close friends Emerson and Thoreau. Sadly, that happiness was short-lived as Elizabeth, the youngest child, grew worse from the lingering effects of scarlet fever, which she had contracted a few years earlier. Louisa, looking back at the year in November 1857, recorded her feelings: "Twenty-five this month. I feel my quarter of a century rather heavy on my shoulders just now. I lead two lives. One seems gay with plays, etc., the other very sad,—in Betty's room; for though she wishes us to act, and loves to see us get ready, the shadow is there, and Mother and I see it."[35] Elizabeth died on March 14, 1858. Louisa wrote to her cousin a few days later, informing her of the sad event: "Last Friday night after suffering much all day, she asked to lie in Father's arms & called us all about her holding our hands & smiling at us as she silently seemed to bid us good bye. . . . At midnight she said 'Now I'm comfortable & so happy,' & soon after became unconscious. We sat beside her while she quietly breathed her life away, opening her eyes to give us one beautiful look before they closed forever."[36] Louisa was greatly affected by her sister's death, and the tragic episode would become the most moving scene in *Little Women*.

Two years later, Alcott lost another sister—this time to marriage. Anna Alcott wed John Bridge Pratt on May 23, 1860. Although Louisa was pleased with the match, she felt the closeknit family was dissolving; those idyllic days of the four sisters together were gone forever. On the wedding day, Louisa dressed in gray—"sackcloth, I called it, and ashes of roses; for I mourn the loss of my Nan, and am not comforted." As the wedding ended, only one consolation presented itself: "Mr. Emerson kissed her [Anna]; and I thought that honor would make even matrimony endurable, for he is the god of my idolatry."[37]

Alcott continued to write for *The Saturday Evening Gazette*, earning ten dollars for each story, but she soon aimed for a higher goal. *The Atlantic Monthly*, begun in 1857, had become the most prestigious literary magazine of the time. Edited by James Russell Lowell and, by 1859, published by Ticknor and Fields, *The Atlantic* was the periodical where every American author wished to place a story, and Alcott was no exception. "Love and Self-Love," her first tale for *The Atlantic*, was published in March 1860. With that accomplishment, Alcott soon completed another story, a tale entitled "A Modern Cinderella," based on the romance of Anna and John Pratt. The piece was accepted for the October 1860 issue, and the proud author received seventy-five dollars: "Emerson praised it, and people wrote to me about it and patted me on the head. Paid bills and began to simmer another."[38]

Men and realities once again intruded as the Civil War broke out in 1861. Alcott confessed in her journal that she had always wanted "to see a war, and now I have my wish. I long to be a man; but as I can't fight, I will content myself with working for those who can."[39] Whatever romantic feelings Alcott possessed about the glory of war were dispelled in early January 1863, when she reported for duty as a nurse at the Union Hotel Hospital in Georgetown,

D.C.: "I never began the year in a stranger place than this; five hundred miles from home, alone among strangers, doing painful duties all day long, . . . surrounded by 3 or 4 hundred men in all stages of suffering, disease & death."[40] At the hospital where the wounded from the battlefields of Virginia constantly streamed in, Alcott herself soon became seriously ill with typhoid fever and was sent home at the end of January, where it took several months for her to regain enough strength to leave her bed.

Alcott wasted little time in turning her real-life experiences into literature, taking the letters she had written to her family from the hospital and publishing them in *The Commonwealth* in the late spring of 1863. By the end of the year, the letters were printed in book form as *Hospital Sketches*, by James Redpath, a noted abolitionist in Boston. With people thirsting for firsthand accounts from the war front, the book attracted good notices. *The Boston Transcript* said the six sketches were "productions of uncommon merit. . . . Fluent and sparkling in style, with touches of quiet humor and lively wit, relieving what would otherwise be a topic too sombre and sad, they are graphic in description."[41] Alcott herself wrote to Redpath that "we all like the book very much, & I have the satisfaction of seeing my towns folk buying, reading, laughing & crying over it wherever I go."[42] With this successful publication, Alcott had moved a world away from her fairy tales.

Earlier that same year, 1863, Alcott had begun a new literary venture—writing sensational stories for what she called the "penny dreadfuls." The reading public were devouring lurid cliff-hangers filled with melodrama; for the cheap price of ten cents, the growing middle class could indulge their appetite for fantasies of witches, villains, savages, murder, and vice. As early as June 1862, Alcott had written her friend Alfred Whitman with her plans: "I intend to illuminate the Ledger with a blood & thunder tale as they are easy to 'compoze' & are better paid than moral & elaborate works of Shakespeare, so don't be shocked if I send you a paper containing a picture of Indians, pirates, wolves, bears & distressed damsels in a grand tableau over a title like this 'The Maniac Bride' or 'The Bath of Blood. A thrilling tale of passion.' "[43]

In January 1863, "Pauline's Passion and Punishment," Alcott's sensational tale, was published in *Frank Leslie's Illustrated Newspaper*. The author was rewarded one hundred dollars for the tale, a prize bestowed upon the best story for Leslie's paper. Frank Leslie, an enterprising force in the New York publishing scene, printed a variety of cheap newspapers; most focused on sensationalism and melodrama and featured graphic illustrations. Alcott had found a lucrative home for her literary efforts, and for the next four years many more of her potboilers would follow in Leslie's periodicals: "A Marble Woman: or, The Mysterious Model"; "Behind a Mask: or, A Woman's Power"; "A Whisper in the Dark"; "A Double Tragedy. An Actor's Story"; "The Freak of a Genius." Most of these tales, which earned Alcott fifty or seventy-five dollars apiece, were published anonymously, or under a pseudonym, such as A. M. Barnard. In an interview, Alcott once confessed that "I think my natural ambition is for the lurid style. I indulge in gorgeous fancies and wish that I dared inscribe them upon my pages and set them before the public." She claimed, she felt "a wretched victim" to the staid village of Concord: "And my favorite characters! Suppose they went to cavorting at their own sweet will, to the infinite horror of dear Mr. Emerson, who never imagined a Concord person as walking off a plumb line stretched between two pearly clouds in the empyrean. . . . And what would my own good father think of me?"[44] Alcott knew these pieces paid the bills for the "pathetic family," but she herself declared them "sensational rubbish."[45] Like her early stories, these blood-and-thunder tales, too, would find their way into *Little Women* as young Jo March submits tales to the *Weekly Volcano*. Just as Alcott did in her own sensational stories, the aspiring author Jo "went abroad for her characters and scenery, and banditti, counts, gypsies, nuns, and duchesses appeared upon her stage and played their part with as much accuracy and spirit as could be expected."[46]

By late 1863, Alcott was also at work on a novel entitled *Moods*, which revolves around a young woman, Sylvia Yule, who marries but realizes too late that she loves another man. The book would occupy her thoughts for over a year, and in September 1864, she gave the manuscript to her friend Caroline Dall, who showed it to the publisher

A. K. Loring. Loring admired the work but also suggested a number of revisions, with which Alcott complied. *Moods* was published in late 1864 and received mixed reviews from the critics. Alcott herself was so dissatisfied with the novel that she would revise it heavily later in her career. The publisher, however, had given Alcott some important advice, telling her that "stories of the *heart* are what live in the memory" and if the author were to "move readers to tears," she would win him.[47]

Alcott listened keenly to Loring's advice, and her fiction would soon capture the hearts of thousands of readers and live for years in their memories. In September 1867, Alcott made the now-famous entry in her journal: "Niles, partner of Roberts, asked me to write a girls book. Said I'd try."[48] Thomas Niles, a native of Boston, had joined the publishing firm of Roberts Brothers in 1863. For the previous fifteen years, Niles had worked as a clerk in the Old Corner Bookstore in Boston, where he had come into contact with many of the most important writers in America: Nathaniel Hawthorne, Ralph Waldo Emerson, Henry Wadsworth Longfellow, Oliver Wendell Holmes. With that valuable experience, he soon became the all-important key behind the success of Roberts Brothers.

By May 1868, Alcott was busy working on *Little Women*, "though I don't enjoy this sort of thing. Never liked girls or knew many, except my sisters; but our queer plays and experiences may prove interesting, though I doubt it."[49] In June, Alcott was still unsure of the merits of the work, but she continued since she felt "lively, simple books are very much needed for girls, and perhaps I can supply the need."[50] Niles himself, however, was certain of the novel's potential and wrote to Alcott in July 1868 that he had "read the whole of it & I am sure it will 'hit', which means I think it will sell well."[51]

Upon Niles's advice, Alcott turned down Roberts Brothers' offer of one thousand dollars for the copyright to *Little Women*. Much later, in 1885, Alcott added a note to the margin of her journal: "An honest publisher and a lucky author, for the copyright made her fortune, and the 'dull book' was the first golden egg of the ugly duckling."[52] She also reluctantly followed his advice to hint at a sequel; thus, the publication ended on an anticipatory note: "So grouped, the curtain falls upon Meg, Jo, Beth, and Amy. Whether it ever rises again, depends upon the reception given to the first act of the domestic drama called 'LITTLE WOMEN.' "[53] Upon reviewing the proofs of the book, Alcott confessed that the novel "reads better than I expected." It was not "a bit sensational, but simple and true," because her family had "really lived most of it; and if it succeeds that will be the reason of it."[54]

Little Women or Meg, Jo, Beth, and Amy was published in early October 1868. The book immediately attracted an audience, and Alcott found a "little success . . . so inspiring" that she agreed to continue the story of the March family. With the sequel, she could now "launch into the future" instead of remembering her childhood escapades.

However, she also planned to thwart the expectations of readers who had written her "to ask who the little women marry, as if that was the only end and aim of a woman's life." She vowed she would not "marry Jo to Laurie to please any one."[55] In April 1869, *Little Women or Meg, Jo, Beth, and Amy Part Second* was published to critical and popular acclaim, and sold even better than the first part, despite the fact that Jo did not live up to her admirers' marital expectations. Three thousand copies of the book had already been sold in advance, and more were coming off the presses each day. *The National Anti-Slavery Standard* wrote that "one leaves it with the sincere wish that there were to be a third and a fourth part; indeed he wishes he need never part company, with these earnest, delightful people."[56] Alcott had clearly touched the hearts of her readers.

Christmas 1869 proved especially rewarding to Louisa. Roberts Brother sent her a check, along with a note: "At this 'Merry Christmas' time, when the inspiration of your mind is gladdening the hearts and homes of so many thousands, we would not forget the author; and we feel we are but the factors of a public, who quick to recognize the genius displayed in 'Little Women,' where by a 'touch of nature,' you have made the 'whole world kin,' generously enable us to silver line your pocket."[57] Alcott responded with her thanks, writing that after "toiling so many years along the up-hill road, always a hard one to women writers, it is peculiarly grateful to me to find the

way growing easier at last; with pleasant little surprises blos-
soming on either side, and the rough places made smooth
by the courtesy and kindness of those who have proved
themselves 'friends' as well as 'publishers.' "⁵⁸ Alcott's
dream of becoming a professional author had come true—
writing had made her famous and wealthy.

Success continued as she published other domestic novels that captured the essence of childhood in New England
and the spirit of children everywhere: *An Old-Fashioned
Girl* (1870), *Little Men* (1871), *Eight Cousins* (1875), *Rose
in Bloom* (1876), *Under the Lilacs* (1878), and *Jo's Boys*
(1882). She also continued to write short stories for the
popular periodicals of the era, such as *St. Nicholas* and
The Youth's Companion. After she had earned her fee from
the magazines, she gathered the tales together in volumes
such as *Aunt Jo's Scrap-Bag*, six volumes (1872–82); *Proverb
Stories* (1882); *Spinning-Wheel Stories* (1884); and *Lulu's Library*, three volumes (1886–89).

While her writing had earned her comfort and financial
security, it could not protect her from heartbreak. In 1870,
while Alcott was away on a grand tour of Europe, her
brother-in-law, John Bridge Pratt, died, leaving behind a
widow and two young sons. In 1877, her mother, the
model for the beloved Marmee of *Little Women*, passed
away. Two years later, May Alcott Nieriker, her younger
sister, died in Europe, where she was starting a career in
art and beginning a family. May's newborn daughter,
Louisa May Nieriker (Lulu), would come to America to

live with her namesake aunt. In 1882, Bronson Alcott suffered a stroke and would need attention and care for the remainder of his life. Thus, Alcott, in her later years, wrote to support her older sister and her two nephews, her invalid father, and her motherless niece. Alcott's own health steadily declined after 1870, finally causing her to seek solace in a nursing home, Dunreath Place, in Roxbury.

On March 1, 1888, Louisa visited her father at her former residence in fashionable Louisburg Square in Boston. She knew his health was failing fast, and as she knelt at his bedside, she grasped his hands and, according to her sister Anna, said, "Father, here is your Louy, what are you thinking of as you lie here so happily?" He took her hand and pointed upward, saying, "I am going *up. Come with me.*" Louisa sadly replied, "Oh, I wish I could."[59] She left for Dunreath Place in her carriage, forgetting her wrap. Upon her return, she immediately became ill and feverish, never learning that her father, with whom she shared the same birthdate, died peacefully in his sleep on March 4. Two days later, March 6, 1888, Louisa May Alcott died. Thomas Niles wrote to her two nephews that she would "be missed and mourned by countless thousands."[60]

In 1853, upon reading one of her stories, the Boston publisher James T. Fields had advised Alcott to "stick to your teaching; you can't write."[61] A year later, Alcott would publish her first book, and seven years later, one of her stories would appear in Field's own magazine, *The Atlantic Monthly*. As a writer, Alcott had progressed from the sentimental romance of *The Inheritance* to the fairy tales of *Flower Fables* to the lurid blood-and-thunder thrillers and to the classic domestic novels of the Little Women series. Between the publication of the first part of *Little Women* in 1868 and the sale of the firm in 1898, Roberts Brothers printed 1,727,551 copies of Alcott's books.[62] By 1947, *Little Women* alone would reach sales of more than two million copies.[63] Alcott indeed had achieved, as her father had hoped upon her birth, "a place in the estimation of society."

NOTES TO THE INTRODUCTION

1. Louisa May Alcott, *Little Women* (1869) (New York: Penguin, 1989), p. 143.

2. Joel Myerson and Daniel Shealy, "The Sales of Louisa May Alcott's Books," *Harvard Library Bulletin* New Series 1 (Spring 1990), p. 67.

3. Michael Anesko, *"Friction with the Market": Henry James and the Profession of Authorship* (New York: Oxford University Press, 1986), p. 176.

4. G. Thomas Tanselle, "The Sales of Melville's Books," *Harvard Library Bulletin* 18 (April 1969), p. 199.

5. Amos Bronson Alcott, *The Letters of A. Bronson Alcott*, ed. Richard L. Hernstadt (Ames, Iowa: Iowa State University Press, 1969), p. 20.

6. Louisa May Alcott, *The Selected Letters of Louisa May Alcott,* ed. Joel Myerson and Daniel Shealy; assoc. ed. Madeleine B. Stern (Boston: Little, Brown, 1987), p. 7.

7. Bronson Alcott, *Observations on the Principles of Infant Instruction* (Boston: Carter and Hendee, 1830), pp. 26–27.

8. *Little Women*, p. 259.

9. Ralph Waldo Emerson, *The Journals and Miscellaneous Notebooks of Ralph Waldo Emerson*, ed. William H. Gilman et al (Cambridge: Harvard University Press, 1961–1975), vol. 8, p. 433.

10. Louisa May Alcott, *The Journals of Louisa May Alcott*, ed. Joel Myerson and Daniel Shealy; assoc ed. Madeleine B. Stern (Boston: Little, Brown, 1989), p. 47.

11. Louisa May Alcott, "Recollections of My Childhood," *Lulu's Library*, vol. 3 (Boston: Roberts Brothers, 1889), pp. 12–13.

12. "Recollections of My Childhood," p. 15.

13. Ibid., p. 15.

14. *The Selected Letters of Louisa May Alcott*, p. 238.

15. *The Journals of Louisa May Alcott*, pp. 63–64.

16. Anna Alcott Pratt, "A Foreword by Meg," *Comic Tragedies. Written by "Jo" and "Meg," and acted by the "Little Women"* (Boston: Roberts Brothers, 1893), p. 7.

17. "Recollections of My Childhood," p. 20.

18. Ibid., p. 16.

19. "A Foreword by Meg," p. 12.

20. See "A Note on the Text."

21. All quotes are from this edition of *The Inheritance*.

22. Herbert Ross Brown, *The Sentimental Novel in America 1789–1860* (New York: Pageant Books, 1959), p. 104.

23. Quoted in Caroline Ticknor, *Hawthorne and His Publisher* (Boston: Houghton Mifflin, 1913), p. 141.

24. M. H. Abrams, *A Glossary of Literary Terms*, 6th ed. (Fort Worth, Tex.: Harcourt, Brace Jovanovich, 1985), p. 191.

25. Brown, p. 133.

26. Ibid., pp. 142–143.

27. Ibid., p. 150.

28. Howard W. Fulweiler, *"Here a Captive Heart Busted": Studies in the Sentimental Journey of Modern Literature* (New York: Fordham University Press, 1993), p. 72.

29. *Little Women*, p. 484.

30. Louisa May Alcott, "The Rival Painters: A Tale of Rome," *The Selected Fiction of Louisa May Alcott*, ed. Daniel Shealy, Madeleine B. Stern, and Joel Myerson (Boston: Little, Brown, 1990), pp. 5–9.

31. *The Journals of Louisa May Alcott*, p. 67.

32. *The Saturday Evening Gazette* (Boston), 23 December 1854, p. 2.

33. *The Selected Letters of Louisa May Alcott*, p. 11.

34. Ibid., p. 60.

35. *The Journals of Louisa May Alcott*, p. 86.

36. *The Selected Letters of Louisa May Alcott*, p. 33.

37. *The Journals of Louisa May Alcott*, p. 99.

38. Ibid., p. 100.

39. Ibid., p. 105.

40. Ibid., p. 113.

41. Quoted in *Critical Essays on Louisa May Alcott*, ed. Madeleine B. Stern (Boston: G. K. Hall, 1984), p. 25.

42. *The Selected Letters of Louisa May Alcott*, p. 88.

43. Ibid., p. 79.

44. LaSalle Corbell Picket, *Across My Path: Memories of People I Have Known* (New York: Brentano's, 1916), pp. 107–108.

45. *The Journals of Louisa May Alcott*, p. 130.

46. *Little Women,* p. 348.

47. Quoted in *Publishers for Mass Entertainment in Nineteenth Century America*, ed. Madeleine B. Stern (Boston: G. K. Hall, 1980), p. 192.

48. *The Journals of Louisa May Alcott*, p. 158.

49. Ibid., pp. 165–166.

50. Ibid., p. 166.

51. Quoted in "The Sales of Louisa May Alcott's Books," p. 50.

52. *The Journals of Louisa May Alcott*, p. 166.

53. *Little Women*, p. 235.

54. *The Journals of Louisa May Alcott*, p. 166.

55. Ibid., p. 167.

56. *The National Anti-Slavery Standard* 29 (May 1, 1869), p. 3.

57. Quoted in "The Sales of Louisa May Alcott's Books," p. 52.

58. *The Selected Letters of Louisa May Alcott*, p. 129.

59. Ibid., p. 337.

60. Quoted in "The Sales of Louisa May Alcott's Books," p. 65.

61. *The Journals of Louisa May Alcott*, p. 109.

62. "The Sales of Louisa May Alcott's Books," p. 68.

63. Frank Luther Mott, *Golden Multitudes: The Story of Best Sellers in the United States* (New York: Macmillan, 1947), p. 102.

SUGGESTIONS FOR
FURTHER READING

Alcott, Louisa May. *Alternative Alcott*, ed. Elaine Showalter. New Brunswick, N.J.: Rutgers University Press, 1988.

———. *Fairy Tales and Fantasy Stories*, ed. Daniel Shealy. Knoxville, Tenn.: University of Tennessee Press, 1992.

———. *The Journals of Louisa May Alcott*, ed. Joel Myerson and Daniel Shealy; assoc. ed. Madeleine B. Stern. Boston: Little, Brown, 1989.

———. *Louisa May Alcott Unmasked: Collected Thrillers*, ed. Madeleine B. Stern. Boston: Northeastern University Press, 1995.

———. *Selected Fiction*, ed. Daniel Shealy, Madeleine B. Stern, and Joel Myerson. Boston: Little, Brown, 1990.

———. *The Selected Letters of Louisa May Alcott*, ed. Joel Myerson and Daniel Shealy; assoc. ed. Madeleine B. Stern. Boston: Little, Brown, 1987.

Anderson, William. *The World of Louisa May Alcott*. New York: HarperCollins, 1995.

Anthony, Katharine. *Louisa May Alcott*. New York: Alfred A. Knopf, 1938.

Barton, Cynthia H. *Transcendental Wife: The Life of Abigail May Alcott*. Lantham, Md.: University Press of America, 1996.

Bedell, Madelon. *The Alcotts: Biography of a Family*. New York: Clarkson N. Potter, 1980.

Cheney, Ednah D. *Louisa May Alcott: Her Life, Letters, and Journals*. Boston: Roberts Brothers, 1889.

Dahlstrand, Frederick C. *Amos Bronson Alcott: An Intellectual Biography*. Rutherford, N.J.: Farleigh Dickinson University Press, 1982.

Delamar, Gloria T. *Louisa May Alcott and "Little Women": Biography, Critique, Publications, Poems, Songs and Contemporary Relevance*. Jefferson, N.C.: McFarland, 1990.

Elbert, Sarah. *A Hunger for Home: Louisa May Alcott and Little Women*. Philadelphia: Temple University Press, 1984; rev. ed. as *A Hunger for Home: Louisa May Alcott's Place in American Culture*. New Brunswick, N.J.: Rutgers University Press, 1987.

Keyser, Elizabeth Lennox. *Whispers in the Dark: The Fiction of Louisa May Alcott*. Knoxville, Tenn.: University of Tennessee Press, 1993.

MacDonald, Ruth K. *Louisa May Alcott*. Boston: Twayne, 1983.

Marsella, Joy A. *The Promise of Destiny: Children and Women in the Short Stories of Louisa May Alcott*. Westport, Conn.: Greenwood, 1983.

Meigs, Cornelia. *Louisa M. Alcott and the American Family Story*. London: Bodley Head, 1970.

Payne, Alma J. *Louisa May Alcott: A Reference Guide*. Boston: G. K. Hall, 1980.

Saxton, Martha. *Louisa May: A Modern Biography of Louisa May Alcott*. Boston: Houghton Mifflin, 1977.

Stern, Madeleine B., ed. *Critical Essays on Louisa May Alcott*. Boston: G. K. Hall, 1984.

———. *Louisa May Alcott*. Norman, Okla.: University of Oklahoma Press, 1950.

Strickland, Charles. *Victorian Domesticity: Families in the Life and Art of Louisa May Alcott*. University, Ala.: University of Alabama Press, 1985.

Ticknor, Caroline. *May Alcott: A Memoir*. Boston: Little, Brown, 1928.

A NOTE ON THE TEXT

The manuscript of *The Inheritance* is at the Houghton Library of Harvard University (★76M-6). The 166-page manuscript of the novel is bound together with the manuscripts of a few other short works by Alcott in reddish orange cloth with a blue spine. Pasted to the inside of the cover is a slip of paper on which Alcott has written "My first novel | written at seventeen | High St   Boston." The manuscript remained with descendants of the Alcott family until it was deposited for safekeeping at Orchard House in Concord, Massachusetts, in the 1930s. The Louisa May Alcott Memorial Association deposited it in 1974 at Harvard, where it was catalogued and made available for researchers.

The manuscript appears to be the final draft of the novel and includes insertions, cancellations, and other revisions. As such, it shows many of Alcott's characteristic traits, such as misspellings (she had particular trouble with "ie" and "ei" words), punctuation marks placed outside quotation marks, incomplete word formations, and grammatical infelicities. Also, the present Chapter 8 appears out of sequence at the end of the novel, where it is, nevertheless, numbered correctly.

In editing Alcott's text, we have corrected obvious spelling and grammatical errors, styled her punctuation according to modern usage, normalized her paragraphing practices, and moved the present Chapter 8 to its proper position in the novel (and renumbered the chapters that follow it). In addition, we have emended some words and phrases that were redundant or unclear, usually by deleting them or restoring earlier readings from the manuscript. Readers wishing to trace our editorial decisions may consult the genetic-text transcription of the manuscript—which presents the text exactly as Alcott wrote it, including insertions and cancellations—deposited at the Houghton Library. In general, we have tried to present a text that would represent Alcott's own intentions had she prepared a revised, clean copy of her manuscript and had it copyedited for publication.

THE INHERITANCE

Chapter I

In a green park, where troops of bright-eyed deer lay sleeping under drooping trees and a clear lake mirrored in its bosom the flowers that grew upon its edge, there stood Lord Hamilton's stately home, half castle and half mansion. Here and there rose a gray old tower or ivy-covered arch, while the blooming gardens that lay around it and the light balconies added grace and beauty to the old, decaying castle, making it a fair and pleasant home.

The setting sun shone warmly through the high stained windows on a group within, and the summer wind lifted the bright locks of a fair girl who sat weaving garlands on the vine-covered balcony. Beside her stood a young and handsome man, while just within the shadow of the crimson curtain a graceful, dark-eyed lady half reclined among the pillows of a velvet couch. Beside her sat another lady, older and more stately, whose proud, cold face grew milder as she watched the young girl with the flowers.

In a recess at the other end of the large and richly furnished room sat another girl, beautiful indeed, but a

3

deep sadness seemed to shadow her pale face. The sunlight that shone softly on her rich, dark hair, folded round her drooping head, fell also on bright tears in the large, mournful eyes, which looked so sadly at the happy group beyond. Her painting lay before her, but the brushes were untouched and she seemed lost in lonely thoughts.

"I hope Lord Percy will be here before my flowers are withered," said the bright-haired girl. "Dear Arthur, look again; he surely must be near."

"No, Amy, not a sound," replied her brother as he looked along the avenue winding through the park. "I fear he will not come. I shall be truly vexed; I did so want you all to know and love him like myself."

"Tell us something more of his past life. You said it had been a sad one and not without romance," said the lady on the couch.

"Ah, do, 'twill while away the time, and we shall feel less like strangers when we meet. Tell us it, Arthur," cried his sister.

"With pleasure, Amy, and if it please *you*, Lady Mother," he answered, turning to the gray-haired lady by his side.

"Yes, Arthur, I am interested in Lord Percy, for I knew his mother years ago. She was a noble woman, and if her son be like her, I can wish for you no truer, better friend. Tell on, and Amy, love, come place some flowers in Ida's hair; she has left that for your skillful hands to do."

"Well, then, I obey and tell the story as I learned it

from one who knew and loved him well. You know I met him in Rome where I was wandering, sick and lonely, trying to regain my health and spirits before I should return. He was like an elder brother to me, kind and tender as a woman, and soon cheered me up and made my journey so delightful that I was really sorry when we reached England on our homeward way. I visited his home and fine old castle, where his mother leads her quiet, solitary life, caring for no other happiness than doing good and loving Walter. He is now her only son, and well deserves a noble mother's love. From her I learned the story of his life, and this is it.

"He was the eldest son of old Lord Percy, who died while he was but a child, so, with his younger brother, he grew up beneath his mother's care: noble, rich, and highborn. Few could lead so pure a life as he. His brother was his dearest friend, whom he watched over with all a father's tenderness and care; but at last a fair young cousin came to live with them, and both the brothers loved her. Neither knew the other's secret, till Walter, our Lord Percy, heard his brother whisper the dear name in sleep, and then he nobly put away his own joy and strove to win for his younger brother the heart he loved so tenderly himself, and he succeeded. The young lovers were married, and none knew why Walter's cheek grew pale or why he stole away when the happy couple told their joy and tried to cheer his sadness. None save his mother ever knew the sacrifice her noble son had made.

"She told me this, for it happened long ago, and the brother and beloved one are both now dead. And since that time he has never loved again. The happy dream so sadly ended never has returned. Courteous and kind to all, devoted to his aged mother, he has lived; loved, honored, and admired for the generous deeds he has done and the blameless life he has led. If I can deserve the friendship he has given me, I shall be more honored than if I had won the favor of a king. And now my tale is done. How does it please you?"

"I had heard something of it years ago but had forgotten it till now," said his mother. "He is indeed a noble man, and you must prize his friendship, Arthur, and teach us to gain it also. Tears, Amy? And for what, my child?"

"Ah, dear Mama," said Amy as she wiped away the drops that filled her gentle eyes. "It was so beautiful in him to hide his love and make his brother happy. How few men would have done it. Was it not a noble thing, Ida?"

"It was indeed, Amy. But you have not told us, Arthur, is he handsome? Half the romance will be gone if he is not."

"He is not what you ladies might consider handsome" was the gay reply, "but to me his calm, pale face and serious eyes are far more beautiful than mere comeliness and grace of form, for the pure, true heart within shines clearly out and gives a quiet beauty to his face, such as few possess. But, hark, surely those are carriage wheels. Yes, here he comes." And young Lord Hamilton went quickly out to meet his friend. The ladies stood upon the balcony to greet him as he passed, while the young girl who sat alone stole softly from the room.

As the carriage rolled swiftly by, the gentleman within bent gracefully and raised his hat. A few moments passed, and then Lord Percy was announced. When the first greetings were over, Amy looked again at the face that had smiled so kindly on her as he took her hand.

It was calm and pale, as Arthur had said, with dark hair parted on a high, white brow, beneath which shone a pair of clear, soft eyes. He was tall and finely formed, with a certain stately grace that well became him. A quiet smile lit up his face and, as the soft light of the evening sun shone on it, Amy thought a beautiful and noble soul must lie within.

Later in the evening, as they sat by moonlight on the terrace, Lord Percy turned to Arthur, saying, "Hamilton, you promised you would show me the old chapel. Would it not look well in this soft light?"

"A good thought, Percy; let us go. Ladies, you will join us? A visit to the haunted ruins by moonlight would just suit my romantic sister and cousin. Ida, you may be inspired to take a sketch. Can we not tempt you out, Mama?"

Lady Hamilton declined, and their gay voices soon died away as they passed through the park towards the lake, where stood the ancient chapel. As they drew nearer, the low, sweet tones of an organ finely played sounded through the silent air.

"The spirits that you say haunt the old chapel are most musical tonight," said Lord Percy as they listened. "Can we not go in and witness their ghostly rites?"

"Yes," replied his friend. "But tread lightly and speak low, for spirits are most timid things, and we must see and yet not be seen ourselves. This way through the porch."

They entered softly and looked up to the gallery whence the music came. The moonlight shone in clear and bright and fell upon the lovely face of the young girl who had stolen away before Lord Percy came. Her soft, dark eyes, no longer filled with tears, were lifted to the light that streamed so brightly in, while her clear, rich voice mingled with the solemn music as she sang an evening hymn.

"It is Edith," whispered Arthur to his sister as they stood together in the shadow of an arch. "How came she here? And how divinely she is singing. Look at Percy. He's a judge of music, and it must be fine for him to listen to it as he does. Stand still and do not call her; it might frighten and disturb her."

So silently they stood till the music died away. Then, rising, the fair singer glided down the narrow stairs and disappeared. Then Lord Percy turned to Arthur, saying with a smile, "I envy you your spirits, Hamilton, if all are as beautiful as this and sing as charmingly. Few voices could have sung that song so perfectly. But might I inquire who the fair ghost is?"

"As we go round the chapel I will tell you, Percy. Edith Adelon is an Italian girl my father brought from Italy when but a child as playmate for my sister. He was touched by her lonely, friendless situation, for her mother had died and her father was unknown. Her beauty, gentleness, and lovely voice all won his heart, and so he brought the homeless child to England. As Amy's faithful friend, she has grown up to womanhood beautiful and richly gifted. Though she is poor and friendless, we all love her for her gentleness and tender care of Amy, to whom she teaches music, painting, and Italian, and better lessons still in patience, purity, and truth. This is her story. How we chanced to find her here I cannot tell, unless she is given to moonlight wanderings like ourselves. Now we must go, for it is damp and chilly. We will come again by daylight, and I'll show you the old tombs."

Lord Percy listened silently, and then, conversing gaily, they went through the moonlit porch to the balcony again.

Chapter II

Lady Hamilton, the widowed mother of Lord Arthur and his sister, was a stern and haughty woman whose whole happiness was in her children, and to them alone did her cold heart warm and all its tenderness and love flow forth. Proud of her broad lands and almost boundless wealth, and prouder still of her high name, she rarely showed affection for any save her kindred. She was not cruel nor unkind to those beneath her, but cold and haughty; and her children, while they feared her, still loved her tenderly. To them she was a fond and faithful mother.

Arthur, the young heir of his dead father's name and wealth, was a frank, warm-hearted youth, kind, generous, and noble. All loved and honored him as one who well became the name he bore. His gentle sister Amy, a gay and lovely girl whose life was all a summer day, he loved most truly; and she returned his love with all her heart, looking up to him and admiring him with all a sister's pride and fond affection.

Lady Ida Clare, the niece of Lady Hamilton, had

inherited her pride and coldness without the hidden tenderness her aunt possessed. Though beautiful and brilliant,
she was still unmarried, for her proud heart longed for rank
and wealth, and few would give her these. Though highborn and lovely, she was poor and from her aunt received
all she possessed. Haughty in spirit, Lady Ida Clare longed
for freedom from dependence; yet though many had admired her, no one had offered more. With bitter disappointment, she saw year after year go by. Her beauty was
fast fading, and her vain and passionate heart mourned this
most deeply, and thus she envied Edith's beauty, youth,
and grace and would almost have consented to sell her
noble name to purchase these. Every look of admiration,
every word of courtesy or kindness given to the gentle girl
she coveted and felt that 'twas Edith's loveliness alone that
won them for her, and so with unkind words and cold
neglect she tried to revenge herself on Edith and her
beauty.

Ida's unkindness was soon felt and her deep dislike
plainly showed. But Edith never guessed the cause, and in
her gentle heart, she longed to win Ida's love and be as
true a friend to her as she had been to Amy. Never by a
reproachful look or a complaining word did Edith betray
how deeply she was pained by the cruelty of one who
should have scorned to injure and insult her poverty and
humble birth.

With an angel's calm and almost holy beauty, Edith
bore within as holy and as pure a heart—gentle, true, and

tender. Few could bear the burden of a lonely life as patiently as she. Longing daily more and more for tenderness and love, she hid the wish deep in her lonely heart. None could tell the wealth of warm affections sleeping there, or with what grateful care a gentle word was cherished or a loving look was remembered, and thus she lived happily in the home they had given and the friendship she had won. Amy truly loved and honored her for all her faithful care and silent deeds of charity that Edith never dreamed were known, and she never knew how she was winning reverence and love from Amy and her brother.

Lord Percy's story has been told, and all his young friend's praises were deserved. Careless of the wealth and honor that might be his, he prized far more the purity and worth of noble human hearts, little noting whether they beat in high or low. Forgetful of the title that he bore, he went among the suffering and the poor and won from them their gratitude and love, which brought a happiness that all the flattery of the great could never give.

The bright dream of his youth had passed away and left within his heart a tender longing and a hope that one day the sweet vision might return and he might win a beautiful and noble wife to cheer life's pilgrimage and bless him with her love. Thus he had mingled in the gay and busy world, and though many lovely faces smiled and gentle voices sounded in his ear, none ever charmed him like his early love, and he had never found the strong, pure heart he sought for.

And now he had come to spend the summer days with young Lord Hamilton. Silently he studied the various characters around him, and in the pure, pale face of the Italian girl he found a charm that daily pleased him more and more, for in it he could read the history of a gentle, patient heart.

Chapter III

The next day passed, and again the evening sun shone on the same group as the night before. Lady Hamilton sat calm and stately in her carved old-fashioned chair, her niece arranged upon the couch so that the crimson curtains threw a rosy light on her dark cheek and the velvet cushions made her arm appear whiter still, with the jeweled bracelet clasped upon it.

Amy, on a low seat at her mother's knee, and Arthur, leaning on the high back of his mother's chair, relaxed, while Lord Percy stood with folded arms beside the open window, telling them in his low, musical voice of Italy and the lovely things there seen.

"They are all beautiful," he said, "but the fairest thing I saw while there was a little flower sent from England, and as I looked on that, paintings, temples, statues, and Italian skies all vanished; and the tender flower was to me more beautiful than all."

"Because some fair hand sent it to you, perhaps, my lord," said Lady Ida with a meaning glance.

"The hand of her who is dearest to me on the earth, my mother," he replied, with a smile that lit up his pale face with a gentle light. "Do you remember how you wondered at my keeping it, Arthur?" he continued. "It is here still." And taking from his bosom a small medallion, he handed it to Lady Hamilton and said, as he removed the little faded flower, "You remember her when young? It is my mother as she is looking now."

"How beautiful," said Amy as she held the picture. "And how much it is like you," she innocently added.

"Thank you for the compliment. I should ask no greater if I resembled her in all things as in this," he answered with a playful bow.

"Whose portrait then is this? A sister's?" asked Amy, as in her confusion she had touched a spring and the medallion flew open, showing a most lovely face of a young and blooming girl.

Lord Percy grew a little paler and his voice was lower as he answered, "Yes, my sister, for she was my brother's wife, and pure as she was beautiful and young," he added. With a sad, sweet smile, he closed the case and laid it in its resting place again.

Amy's warm heart beat, and tears were in her eyes as she remembered how he had loved and suffered for her whose picture she had just seen and how he still treasured it when she was dead.

Arthur understood Lord Percy's sigh and Amy's silence, and to cheer them both he gaily said, "Amy here would prize a flower from Italy as you do yours, Percy, for it is her chosen country, and I have promised her a trip to Rome when she has done with lessons and can go without Mama."

"Well, Arthur, you may jest with me about it, but how can I help loving the land that one so dear and good as Edith calls her home?" said Amy. "Ah, if you could listen to the tales she tells and hear the sweet songs she can sing of it, you would not wonder that I long to journey there."

"Our Saint Cecilia of last night you speak of?" said Lord Percy. "Yes, when Italy can send you such a voice as that, you may well love it; but does she never sing to any but yourself, Lady Amy?"

"Not often, but tonight she may come down and sing to us, may she not, Mama? Cousin Ida has not touched her harp all day, and I am weary of my own songs. Let me call her. She will gladly come if I but ask her."

"No, my love; ring the bell and bid the footman ask Miss Adelon to join us," replied her mother, adding in a lower tone, "You must remember, Amy, that your governess can never mingle with the friends who visit you. *She* is poor and lowborn; *you* are Amy Hamilton."

"Yes, Mama," said Amy, "but it's strange that one so beautiful and good should be shut out from all she would enjoy so much. Ah, here she comes."

A light step sounded through the room, and then Edith stood by Lady Hamilton, saying in a low voice, "What are your wishes, madam?"

"You will sing to us, if you please. Take Lady Ida's harp and place it there." She coldly waved her hand.

Edith was turning away when Arthur, with true courtesy, said, "Lord Percy, this is Amy's friend, Miss Adelon." She gracefully returned his salutation and passed on to the harp.

Lady Ida frowned, for she had seen that Lord Percy bowed as low to the humble governess as he had done to her, the highborn niece of Lady Hamilton. "What do you prefer, my lord? Miss Adelon will play whatever you may choose."

"Might I ask the evening hymn my mother used to sing? It is the song I love the best," he answered, turning to Edith as he spoke. With a smile, she touched the harp and, as her low, sweet voice sounded through the silent room, Amy watched Lord Percy, who bent his head and listened silently, though Lady Ida talked and rustled with her fan. When the song was done and he looked up, she saw his eyes were full of tears. "His mother sang it," thought she, "and how well he loves it."

Song after song was called for, and each seemed sweeter than the last.

"Ought we to ask for more?" at length Lord Percy said as he heard a low sigh when she ceased. "Beautiful as it is, it must be wearisome to her."

"You need sing no more," said Lady Ida haughtily. "We are tired of it now."

The young girl rose and, as she passed, a flower that

had been placed in her dark hair fell out. Lord Percy stooped and raised it, saying with a smile, "Miss Adelon's music is the sweetest I have heard since I left Italy, her native land." The clear, soft eyes, raised to his as she took the flower, filled with tears as he spoke of Italy. With a gentle "Thank you," she passed out through the door he opened for her.

Lady Ida bit her lip, for her fan had been lying just before him, and he had not thought to take it up. "Does she not sing charmingly?" cried Amy. "Do you not think it very sweet?"

He started and replied, "She is indeed most beautiful."

"Where are your thoughts, Percy? Amy asked your opinion of her music and you reply she is very lovely," said Arthur, laughing.

"I beg your pardon, Lady Amy," he replied, while the color deepened in his cheek. "She has a most uncommon voice. Where did she learn to sing?"

"Her mother was an opera singer, I believe," said Lady Ida, "and Edith might be, too, if it were not for my uncle's care."

"Oh, Ida, that could never be," cried Amy. "She has told me that her mother was an Italian lady, poor indeed but of good family, and that you might know by Edith's grace and beauty."

"So that is the story that she tells," said Lady Ida with an unbelieving smile. "It is a good one, and you believe it, do you, Amy?"

"She would not be my sister if she doubted Edith's word," said Arthur warmly. "Edith is of a good, perhaps a noble family, for there is a dignity and highborn look about her that would become any lady in the land. Now, Percy, we will go to the library and I will show you the books I spoke of." And, breaking off the conversation, Arthur led his friend away, and Lady Ida, who had planned a stroll with Lord Percy, was left to her angry feelings and disappointed hopes.

Chapter IV

The pleasant summer days went gaily by to the young party, who rode and rambled to their hearts' content. Lord Percy was kind and attentive, and Lady Ida was happy. Amy and her brother often longed for Edith to enjoy their pleasure with them, but she always managed to avoid it, sitting alone in her quiet chamber or walking beside the lake in solitary sadness.

"The carriage will be at the door in an hour, Amy, and we must be off to the crags. Percy is a lover of fine scenery, and this shall be our next excursion. Remember your sketchbook, Cousin Ida, and Edith will sing us her sweetest songs as we wander like babes in the wood," said Arthur gaily as he joined them one bright and sunny afternoon.

"Is Miss Adelon to be of the party? That's an unexpected honor," said Lady Ida in a tone of scornful surprise.

"Oh, yes, Mama," cried Amy, "half the pleasure of the ride is lost to me if Edith is not there. She is so fond of lovely things. Oh, do say yes, Mama."

"As you please, my love. How can I refuse to make you happy? She may go if Ida is willing."

"Ah, yes," Ida carelessly replied, "we shall need someone to take our shawls as we walk up the rocks. The servants would not care to do it."

Lord Percy, who had been standing near her, turned quietly, saying, "Nay, Lady Ida, that we gentlemen shall claim as one of our high honors if we may."

He had seen the color rise to Edith's cheek and heard Amy whisper, "Dear Ida, be more kind," and he resolved to learn the cause of Amy's love and Lady Ida's deep dislike of the fair Italian girl whose beauty, grace, and friendless lot had touched his generous heart and won his pity.

He little thought that Lady Ida, jealous of Edith's loveliness and rare accomplishments, had learned to hate her for the charms which she so longed to call her own and that she vented her dislike in scornful words and little slights to try and trouble Edith's gentle spirit. In time, however, he learned all this, and it but deepened the interest he felt in the orphan girl.

Through the green old park rolled the barouche while Lord Percy and his young host on horseback rode before. The summer sun shone brightly and the cool wind blew freshly by, leaving a rosier bloom on Amy's cheek as she sat beside her friend, whose calm and thoughtful face formed a sweet contrast to the blooming, girlish one beside her.

Lady Ida, leaning out, seemed to be enjoying the lovely

scenes through which they passed, but her eye rested only on the stately figure of Lord Percy, as with uncovered head he rode beneath the drooping trees. The soft wind stirred his waving hair; the cheerful sunshine brought a clearer light to his dark eyes and Arthur's jests a gayer smile to his lips. As she watched, stronger grew the wish within her that she might win so pure and true a heart and be the first to fill the place left vacant by his early love. He was high-born, rich, and noble; her ambitious heart could ask no more. She knew he would not care for her lack of wealth, and none before had ever done so; and secretly she resolved to win what all others failed to gain.

"Lord Percy, there they are," cried Lord Hamilton as they drew near the lofty pile of rocks they were to visit. "We pride ourselves upon our crags and think no view in England half so beautiful as that we see when standing on their highest peak. Perhaps," he added with a laugh, "it is because the broad lands lying just beneath belong to us, and who does not like to look upon his wealth, however small it be."

"They are indeed a noble pile," replied Lord Percy, "and well worth the ride to look upon them. But here we must dismount, I think you said, and take this narrow path to reach the top."

"My lord, I shall trust myself to you," said Lady Ida as she stepped from the carriage, "and in return for the support of your arm I will lead you to the point from which the best view may be obtained. Arthur, take good care of

Amy. She is like an uncaged bird when in the woods. And now, let our procession move." And with her sweetest smile, she placed her hand within his offered arm and, talking gaily, led the way along the narrow path. "What have you lost, my lord?" she asked when they had gone a little way, observing that her companion often looked behind. "The crags are just before us, and there are Arthur and Amy halfway up. We must not let them gain the top before us."

"I was looking for Miss Adelon," he said. "She was alone and might not know the way. The rocks are dangerous. Shall we not wait for her?"

"Oh, no," said Lady Ida with a scornful smile. "She has been here before and likes to be alone and wander in the woods, as most romantic governesses do. She will overtake us by the time we reach the cliff. Come, let us hasten on, my lord."

With another glance behind, he obeyed and soon stood beside young Hamilton and his sister on the gray old rock, looking down on river, field, and grove for miles around.

"How freshly the wind blows," said Lady Ida as she looked along the path up which they had come. "What can keep Edith? How can she linger so when I want my shawl?"

"I will go and bring it, Lady Ida," said Lord Percy, and before she could detain him, he had hastened down the rock.

Edith, left alone, went slowly on, enjoying the sunlight

and the air, forgetting all neglect and coldness in the lovely things around her. She was trying to reach a spray of sweet wild flowers that grew above her when a hand bent down the branch and broke the thorny bough, while a gentle voice beside her said, "Will Miss Adelon allow me to add this to her bouquet and see her safely up the rocks?"

She turned and saw Lord Percy smiling kindly with the roses in his hand. "Thank you, my lord," she said. "I fear I have kept them waiting, but the flowers have rendered me forgetful that I might be needed." And she hastened up the path.

"Let me share your burden," said Lord Percy as he walked beside her. "The flowers I'll yield to you, but these are mine." And he removed the shawls she carried, adding gently, "Could not the footman take these for you? One needs to be free and unencumbered climbing up these rocks."

"Lady Ida bid the footman stay behind, and so I brought them," she answered with a sigh of weariness. "See, she is beckoning. I have done wrong to linger so."

"Nay, do not tire yourself with hastening on so fast, Miss Adelon. If you come but seldom, you should enjoy it while here. Do you not go out with Lady Amy when she rides?" he asked.

"When she goes alone, I am her companion, but I seldom see so beautiful a scene as this, and in my happiness I have forgot my duty."

"How few joys she must have if this can give her such

great happiness," thought Lord Percy as he looked down on the fair face at his side. The faint, soft color in her cheek and the smile upon her lips, half hidden by her falling hair, and the clear, dark eyes so bright with inward joy, all made her lovelier than when he saw her pale and sad amid the smiling faces that surrounded him. In his kind heart he resolved that though others might neglect and slight her, he would give her all the courtesy and reverence he paid the noble and the rich. With respectful care, he led her up the rough, uneven path and stood before Lady Ida with the shawls on one arm and Edith on the other.

Though angry at his absence and his kindness to the girl she so disliked, Lady Ida smiled and thanked him and then began to sketch Lord Hamilton. His friend stood beside her, and Edith with Lady Amy wandered here and there gathering flowers.

"This is beautiful, Ida," said her cousin when she handed him the sketch. "Every rock and tree are perfect. Look, Percy, is it not fine?"

"It is indeed a faithful copy of the wild scenery about us. That old shattered tree is excellent, but why not add the figure that is leaning there? She is beautiful enough to grace your picture," said Percy as he pointed to Edith, who was standing by the old tree. Her hands were folded and her long locks, lifted by the breeze, showed that her tearful eyes were looking fondly to the distant hills beyond which lay her native land.

"I should have done so," said Lady Ida as she closed

her book, "but she had placed herself there and in that attitude to attract our attention. It is all affectation, I assure you."

A faint smile crossed Lord Percy's face as he glanced at the speaker, who reclined upon the rock in an attitude of the most studied grace.

"No, Ida," cried Arthur, "you wrong her. She is as natural and unaffected as she is beautiful and good. Edith is a noble girl, and were it not for my mother, I would gladly offer her a higher place in my home, and she should be to Amy as a sister, for she has been a faithful friend."

"I honor you for it, Arthur," said Lord Percy. "Purity and truth are seldom found, and when they are, we should admire and honor them wherever they may be and for themselves alone."

"Should we not be going?" said Lady Ida as she rose. "Lady Arlington may have arrived, and we should be there to meet them."

"What's that?" cried Arthur as a wild cry of pain and terror rang through the silent air.

"It's Amy's voice," said Lady Ida. "Oh, what has happened?" They hurried to the spot whence the cry had come and there found Edith, deadly pale, upon her knees, leaning over the edge of the precipice, whose steep sides sloped far down to the water's edge. Many feet below was Amy, clinging to the roots of a slender vine that grew in a crevice of the rock, her pale face looking up imploringly. Though her white lips moved, no sound was heard.

"How can we save her?" cried Arthur as he wrung his hands in helpless grief. "We cannot reach her! Oh, Percy, must we see her die?"

"Be calm, dear Arthur. Do not frighten her," said his friend as he glanced rapidly up and down the rough, steep cliff. "I will trust to the vines and clamber down. But, no, I cannot reach her. Then God help us now. Is there no way left?"

"Yes," said Edith as she sprang up, "look, there is a narrow ledge that leads to yonder tree. Once there, we could reach her." And she drew nearer to the precipice with a pale cheek but a brave heart beating high within her.

"No, no, you must not go," cried Arthur and Lord Percy as they both detained her. "It will not bear you. You are going to your death."

"Do not stay me," she calmly said. "Amy needs me. I must save her. There are none to grieve if I am lost, but think of her and of your mother and let me go." With one glance at the cloudless heaven and a whispered prayer upon her lips, she had reached the narrow ledge before they could again detain her and, with a firm, light step, passed slowly to the tree that drooped its leafy boughs above the fearful cliff.

They stood in deathlike silence and heard her saying cheerfully, "Look up, dear Amy. I will save you. Place your foot in that little niche and give me your hand."

Amy placed her trembling foot where she was told and, clinging still to the frail vines, stretched up her hand. Edith, holding tightly to the tree, bent down, but, alas, she could not reach her. Arthur then sank upon his knees and could only pray for help.

"Arthur! Arthur! Look up. She has not failed. The brave girl will save her yet. Take courage and look up," cried Lord Percy.

Edith had taken the long scarf from her shoulders and, binding one end firmly to the strongest bough, flung down the other, saying, "Amy, love, seize and hold it fast. It will help you raise yourself till I can reach you. Do not fear. Think of your mother and take heart, dearest."

With the last effort of her failing strength, Amy caught the scarf and drew herself slowly up till Edith, heedless of her own danger, leaning toward her, took her hand and, with a strong arm, raised her to the narrow place where she was standing. Half carrying, half leading the fainting girl, Edith passed along the perilous path and laid Amy safe but senseless in her brother's arms.

"Thank God and you, Edith!" cried Arthur as he bent over her and held the water that Lord Percy had brought to her pale lips. "She breathes again and, see, the color is returning to her cheek. Look up, dear Amy; you are safe."

"Where is Edith?" whispered she as her eyes unclosed. "Did she not come to save me when all hope was gone? She is not hurt? Oh, bring her to me."

"I am here, love," said a low voice at her side. A tearful face bent over her, and loving arms were folded tenderly about her.

"How did it happen, and why were you there alone?" said Lady Ida when they had grown calmer, with an angry glance at Edith.

"Do not blame her, Ida. Had it not been for her, I should not be here now," said Amy with a shudder at the dreadful death she had escaped. "She begged me not to go, but I would try to get a flower that grew in a crevice of the rock and slipped. Oh, it was terrible to be so helpless in such danger. If Edith had not strengthened me by her cheerful words, I should have fallen, and God alone could save me then! How can I ever thank you, dearest Edith, for the dangers which you dared for me?" She wept her gratitude and joy upon the gentle bosom where she lay.

"By being calm and still, dear Amy," whispered Edith. "Weep no more, but lean on me and we will go to carriage and home as quickly as we can."

"You are pale and trembling, Edith; lean on Percy," said Arthur. "Ida and I will take Amy. God bless you," he continued with emotion as he took her hand. "God bless you, Edith. I cannot thank you now, but a day will come when I can show the boundless gratitude I feel. Go slowly, Percy; it is a rough path for these faint limbs. Come, Amy, love."

"There waves the scarf, like a banner telling of a brave

heart's victory over fear and peril," said Lord Percy as they slowly moved away.

"Why do you look so sadly at it, Edith? Do you wish another life risked to get it for you?" said Lady Ida coldly.

"Oh, no," said Edith gently, "I loved it, for it was my mother's, but we must go for Amy's sake, for the dew is falling and it's growing cool." And, with another sad look at the fluttering scarf, she turned away, and on Lord Percy's arm went slowly down the rugged path, wondering at the care with which he bent the branches back and moved the scattered stones away.

They reached the carriage and were driving off when Lord Percy said, "Drive on. I will arrange this bridle and soon overtake you." They drove away and, though Lady Ida watched in the gathering twilight for the horse and its graceful rider, it was not till they were entering the park that Lord Percy joined them.

"What has detained you?" said Arthur from the carriage, where he had taken a seat to support Amy. "We thought the fairies of the rock must have enchanted you."

"Arthur, no questions. If I were to confess how well I love romantic wanderings, I should lose Lady Ida's good opinion. Forever spare me such a loss, and I will only say I was detained," replied Lord Percy gaily. "Tell your mother carefully of Amy's danger, Arthur," he continued as he handed them out.

As Edith entered the hall, a light touch fell upon her

arm, and his low voice said, "A mother's gift is rendered sacred by a daughter's love. I could not let the wind and rain destroy this." And, laying the scarf upon her arm, he passed on, but he heard the faltered thanks and saw the bright tears on the fair face looking up so gratefully to him. The reason of his long delay was now explained and, with a wondering joy, she kissed the rescued gift and thought with fear of the dangerous path he must have gone to reach it.

"My lady waits to see you," said a servant, and, concealing the scarf, Edith hastened to the drawing room.

Amy lay upon the couch, and happy tears were on her pale cheek, for she who had saved her life would now be loved as she had longed to love her. Arthur took Edith's hand, saying as he led her to his mother, "Love her, Mother, for she has well won it."

Lady Hamilton bowed her proud head and kissed the white brow bent before her, saying, "Edith, henceforth you have a new claim on my love and care. You are Amy's governess no longer. Be her sister and her friend."

"Dear Edith, you are ill," cried Amy as she saw her cheek grow pale and a look of suffering cross her face.

"I have strained my arm a little, Amy. That is all. I will retire if you please." And, with a quick step, she passed out.

A moment afterward, a servant entered, saying, "Miss Adelon has fainted in the hall, my lady." Amy, forgetting worries and pain, sprang up, and they all hastened out and found her pale and still upon the marble floor.

Lord Arthur raised her, saying, as he laid her on the couch, "We should have watched more carefully. She must have been suffering in silence all this time, and not by word or sigh has she betrayed it until she could bear no more. She does not yet seem conscious. We must have a doctor. Percy, hold the water to her lips. Why, where is he?"

"Gone for a surgeon, my lord. I told him I would go, but he said I was not fast enough, and he rode away at full speed," said the servant.

"You may go, Robert. This is like him. He would do as much for any poor and suffering creature in the meanest hut," said Arthur as he bent over Edith.

"If she were not young and pretty, I should doubt it, Arthur," said Lady Ida with an incredulous smile. "Few young men would."

"There are but few Lord Percys, Cousin Ida. This self-ish world would be the better were there more. Ah, she is reviving. Bathe her temples, Amy. We will not move her till Doctor Morton comes."

A horse dashed by the window, and in a moment more, Lord Percy entered, saying, "I met the good doctor in the park, and he will be here immediately. Has she recovered?" He took the cold hand in his own and gently chafed it.

"I never can forgive myself for being so forgetful and

unkind. 'Twas lifting me up from that dreadful rock that hurt her arm, and how silently she suffered till she could bear no more. Dear Edith, do you know me?" said Amy as, with a faint sigh, Edith looked about her.

"Yes, love, you are safe. Do not tell them I am hurt. I can bear it till we are at home. This pain is easier to bear than Lady Ida's unkind words."

"She is not herself yet," said Amy as she bent fondly over her to hide the blush that Edith's unconscious words of Ida caused.

"Here is the doctor. Now all will go well," said Arthur as he shook the old man's hand and led him to the couch.

"What's all this?" said he. "You are pale, Lady Amy, and Miss Adelon fainting. What is the trouble, Lady Hamilton? I met my friend Lord Percy riding like a madman, and all I understood was that someone was saved and someone hurt."

Lord Percy, with a smile, now told him all that had occurred. "Ah, yes, a strain, and a pretty serious one to cause a swoon like this. She must be taken to her room directly," said the doctor.

"My lord, do not trouble yourself," said Lady Ida as Lord Percy and Arthur raised her. "The servants can carry Edith."

"It were a poor return for all she has done to leave her to the care of servants now," replied Lord Percy with a look of calm surprise. "Light me, Arthur. I will follow." And, tenderly lifting her, he bore his easy burden up the stairs, and Lady Ida was left alone, for Amy and her mother followed them.

"By this one thing," thought she, "that girl has won a place here that I never dreamed she would. When my aunt stoops to one beneath her as she has tonight, I fear she will raise her higher still, and then I am undone. Lord Percy's admiration she has won by her brave deed today, and that may deepen into love, for she is very lovely, as I know too well. No, no, it shall never be. I'll send her friendless from this house before I will see her placed above me, even by my aunt." And with bitter and revengeful thoughts, the proud woman sought her room.

Chapter V

Several days passed on, and Amy sat beside and tended her friend with unwearied care till she was well again and could resume her quiet seat below, bearing no trace of her illness save a paler cheek and her arm supported by a sling. All kindly welcomed her, and all but Lady Ida showed how much they felt the grateful love they owed her for the brave deed she had done and the silent suffering she had borne. Lady Hamilton was as kind and friendly as so cold and proud a woman could be, while Amy and her brother strove by tender words and every kind attention in their power to make her feel how high a place she had won in their affection and regard. Though Lord Percy never spoke of it, his eye would often rest on the young girl's pale and tranquil face with a deep reverence and silent admiration of the brave heart that beat within her. In his manner towards her there was a gentle courtesy quite different from his calm and graceful ease with Lady Ida, who seemed to appropriate his conversation to herself and in return bestowed her most winning smiles and fascinating words.

When she chose, no one could be more charming, gay, witty, beautiful, and brilliant. Few would guess how selfish and how cold a heart was hers, and Edith, happy in the love she had won, forgot all past unkindness and neglect and daily grew more beautiful and gay.

And thus things went till Lady Arlington and her son arrived, and preparations were made for a fete to be given in honor of Amy's birthday.

"Who was that lovely girl we passed on the lawn as we drove up?" asked Lord Arlington of his young host as they stood on the balcony, where they had assembled, as it was their custom, to watch the sunset and lay plans for tomorrow's pleasures.

"One of the gardener's daughters, I presume," said Lady Ida coldly.

"Hardly that, I think, begging your ladyship's pardon," he replied, "for though simply dressed, there was a graceful elegance about her that led me to suppose she was a visitor, and that was why I asked."

"Oh, then it must be Edith," said Amy. "Had she dark hair and lovely eyes?"

"Yes, very lovely, I assure you. She was a fascinating little object altogether as she stood gathering flowers by the lake. If all the statues in your park, Arthur, were like this one, it would soon be stripped. But who may this mysterious Edith be, if I might ask?"

"A poor Italian girl and Amy's governess," said Lady Ida with a haughty smile.

"Also the preserver of Lady Amy's life and a very beautiful and noble woman," said Lord Percy, who was leaning on the carved stone balustrade watching Edith as she came up through the garden.

"Ah, I forgot you are her chosen champion and wear her colors as a true knight should," said Lady Ida as she glanced at the flower he wore.

"This is Lady Amy's gift and a fitting emblem of its fair and gentle giver," he calmly answered, bowing with a smile to Amy. "But if Miss Adelon should need a champion, where could we find a better cause than in defending innocence and beauty from the dangers of an envious and cruel world? Ah, here she comes like Flora with her flowers," he added.

Edith came along the balcony and laid her well-filled basket at Amy's feet with a playful smile.

"I lay my humble gifts before your highness, queen of our tomorrow's fete, hoping they are worthy of your acceptance."

"How kind of you, dear Edith, to think of gathering them. We need so many garlands for tomorrow," said Amy. "Now sit here and rest while teaching me to weave the lovely wreaths you make with so much skill."

Young Hamilton stepped forward, saying, "Edith, my friend Lord Arlington has heard of your great deeds and longs to know my sister's dearest friend. This is Miss Adelon, Frederick."

With a deep blush at the bold look of admiration the

young man gave her, she returned his bow and, kneeling on the cushion at Amy's feet, began to form a wreath while the conversation was resumed.

"What is the order of performances tomorrow, Arthur?" said Lady Ida as she placed a flower in her bosom.

"Our plan is this," he answered. "The tables for the villagers are to be spread in the park, where they shall drink to dear Amy's health till the ale gives out, and then a dance upon the green shall finish off the fete to them. In the evening we illuminate the grounds and welcome all our friends who choose to come. We will dance and sing, and those romantically disposed like Percy and myself can wander through the park and admire my taste in decorating sober rakes with colored lamps and turning night to day. This is my plan, but if you can suggest any new and striking improvements, I beg you will."

"Why not have boats upon the lake? It would be delightful sailing there by the soft light of the lamps. Could it not be done?" said Amy.

"Queens' wishes are commands. I will give Robert orders that it may be so," said her brother as, with a playful bow, he hastened out.

"How beautiful and how becoming," cried Amy as she placed a wreath of pure white flowers on Edith's head. "Dear Ida, I have often asked you for a sketch. Take Edith as she is and I will never tease again."

"My book and pencils are not here, Amy, and I do not care to send for them," said her cousin coldly.

"They are here. Allow me to bring them to you, Lady Ida," said young Arlington as he took the book from a table just within the window.

"Thank you, but I am too tired now. Another time I will obey you, Amy."

"These flowers will be withered then and the wearer may be gone. Taken now, in this soft light, a lovely picture might be made. Can we not persuade you?" said Lord Percy, offering again the book.

"No, my lord, but why not take the sketch yourself? I know your talent, and if you like Italian faces, Edith's will just suit you," answered Lady Ida as she laid the book aside.

" 'Tis a most tempting offer. How can you resist?" said young Arlington. "I never cared for it before, but I would gladly be a painter now. You surely will not refuse?"

"Miss Adelon's consent should first be won, and then I will gladly give Lady Amy my best sketch of her friend," replied Lord Percy as he looked at Edith for permission.

"Another time, dear Amy, but not now, not here," pled Edith as she took the garland from her hair.

"Nay, you have called me queen, and as my subject I command you to submit. You see what a tyrant you have made me," said Amy as she replaced the wreath. "How shall she stand, my lord?"

"Kneel as she knelt before and go on weaving flowers, if it please your majesty. It was very natural and graceful," said Lord Percy as he placed the paper and began.

"With all your skill you cannot keep the blush, my lord," said young Arlington as he stood beside him watching Edith's crimsoned cheek, half hidden by her hair. "Should not the eyes be raised and turned toward you?"

"She is timid and it were not kind to ask for more; for Lady Amy's sake alone has she consented, and we should respect her too much to give her pain for a picture's sake," replied Lord Percy, adding in a lower tone, "I can remember how the eyes should look."

Lady Ida heard it, and though trying to appear indifferent and careless, she thought she had never seen Edith look more beautiful than now, and in her jealous heart she could not bear to see Lord Percy look so long and earnestly upon her and hear Lord Arlington's whispered admiration of "the loveliest girl he had ever seen."

At length it was done and Lady Amy, as she looked, exclaimed, "Oh, thank you! You have caught her very look and made her as she really is, so beautiful and sweet. See, Edith, is it not like you?"

"Your love, dear Amy, makes your friends fairer than they truly are, but if it pleases you, I shall be happy that it is done" was the gentle answer.

"I will reward you with another flower," said Amy as she took a bud from Edith's wreath and gave it to Lord Percy.

"He doubtless would prefer a copy of the picture, Amy. Painters like to keep all their successful efforts," said

Lady Ida as she carelessly threw by the sketch she had been looking at.

"I can hardly hope for that, though I should like to place it with some other sketches I had made of all the virtues," he replied.

"What would Edith represent?" asked Lady Ida. "Purity?"

"Or Patience," he replied as he saw her meek eyes look reproachfully at Lady Ida, who seemed to lose no opportunity to hurt and try her gentle spirit.

"I have Lady Amy there as Innocence, and why not give her friend a place beside her, and I may venture to include you in the number, if you will honor me," he added with a smile, seeing the frown on Lady Ida's face. And fearing he had offended her, he took a seat beside her, and she soon forgot both Edith and her anger in listening to the voice so musically sounding at her side. The picture was forgotten, but Lord Arlington, while watching the lovely model, had been captivated by her beauty, grace, and simple dignity and had resolved to win her if he could and forget her humble birth by surrounding her with all the charms of rank and wealth.

Young, thoughtless, and gay, he had been spoiled by the world. Now, selfish, passionate, discontented, and tired of the pleasures he had once enjoyed, he was more easily charmed by Edith's pure and gentle nature, for it was new. Therefore, he pursued this pleasing novelty as he did all things, careless of the pain he gave and bent on gaining what he sought. From the hour when he stood looking on as she knelt among the flowers with the rosy evening light upon her pure, pale face, she was ever before him, and he longed to win her more and more.

Chapter VI

The morrow came, and Amy's seventeenth birthday was as bright and beautiful as she herself when crowned with flowers and leaning on her brother's arm. She bowed her thanks to the happy villagers, who waved their hats and drank to her health beneath the trees at the feast so bountifully spread for them.

"This is Edith's table. Come and see her wait upon the children. She never yields her place to anyone, and there she is surrounded by the little ones," said Arthur, pointing to her as she moved among them with a kind word and cheerful smile for all.

"How is your mother, little Jenny?" said Amy to a bright-eyed child, who dropped a curtsy as she answered.

"Almost well, your ladyship, though Father says we owe it all to dear Miss Adelon, who comes through wind and rain each day bringing fruit and wine to Mother and cheers her up by her sweet face and gentle words. She will not let us thank her for her great kindness, so will you tell how grateful we all feel and beg her not to come when she is ill, for often she looks pale and sad," said the child, forgetting her timidity in her earnest wish to show her gratitude and love for her kind friend.

"You can tell her that henceforth your mother will have other friends who will try to be as watchful and unwearied as herself, and she may rest from her silent acts of charity and let us learn of her. Now go and join your playmates, Jenny; we will remember you," said Lord Hamilton. As the child ran gaily off, he turned to his companions, saying, "Did you not tell me, Percy, that you had seen Edith cross the park several times quite early in the morning?"

"Yes. I fancied she was as fond of early rambles as myself and would have gladly borne her basket, which seemed often heavy when her arm was weak, but she seemed to avoid me and I would not annoy her by my presence," replied Lord Percy.

"We must not let her go alone, Amy," said her brother. "She is not strong and often does too much for others, forgetful of herself. We will share her good works and she shall teach us how to win gratitude and love like little Jenny's. Now come to the lake and see the boats you ordered. They are ready for the evening."

Gaily passed the day, and, as sunset faded into twilight and the villagers were gone, a thousand lights gleamed forth among the drooping trees, and music sounded from the balconies as carriage after carriage rolled through the lighted park and left its gay burden on the lawn. Soon throughout the brilliant house and grounds sounded happy voices, and gay parties wandered by.

"Is it not beautiful?" said Amy, glancing round the flower-decked saloon as she stood beside Lord Percy, her partner in the dance. "I am so happy tonight. I fear I shall shock Mama and Lady Arlington by my undignified display of spirits. Ah, there comes Edith with Lord Arlington to join our set. I am glad she has been asked by someone besides Arthur."

"Why?" said Lord Percy.

"Because she is often neglected by the friends who visit us and, loving her as I do, it grieves me to see others slight her because, though beautiful and good, she is poor. You do not feel so, I know, and will you dance with her?" said Amy timidly.

"I have asked her, and for three dances I shall have the pleasure of showing those who slight her that Lord Percy feels honored by the choice of one he respects and admires so sincerely as Miss Adelon," replied he with a smile. Those who heard him speak so earnestly turned to look at Edith and were more courteous and kind to one of whom Lord Percy had so spoken.

"Well, dear Edith, we have a gay evening before us, have we not?" said Amy as her friend joined her, looking so beautiful and bright in her simple ball dress, with no ornaments save flowers in her hair and the rare loveliness of her own sweet face.

"After a hard struggle, I have won her for this dance,"

said Lord Arlington gaily, "but some troublesome person has engaged her for the three next, and if he will not yield, why, I must live on hope till then."

"The troublesome person will not yield on any account," replied Lord Percy with a smile, "unless Miss Adelon prefers a gayer partner than myself."

"I beg your pardon, Percy," said Lord Arlington, laughing, "but it was provoking when I had promised myself the pleasure of Miss Adelon's hand for as many dances as she chooses to honor me with it. But there is the music; we begin."

"Frederick is very attentive to that Miss Adelon," said Lady Arlington to Lady Hamilton as they sat watching the gay scene before them. "I think you told me she was well-born, though poor."

"Yes, Edith is of good birth, though there is a mystery about her parents that has never been explained. She is so lovely that no doubt she will soon win a home for herself. Till then I consider her my charge."

"She does not visit with you, I believe," said Lady Arlington, who felt curious to know why she had never seen Edith before, though she often visited Lady Hamilton.

"She will in the future go wherever Amy goes. She has been her teacher for many years, and by her virtue and fidelity has won a place in all our hearts. Amy's education is now nearly finished, and Edith is to be provided for. She is beautiful and young, and in a home of her own will be

far happier than here. I have told you of her courage in
saving Amy. From that time I have looked upon her as a
friend to whom I owe a debt that I never can repay and,
as a small return for the precious life she saved, I shall do
all I can to make her happy." Lady Hamilton spoke more
kindly than usual, for where her children were concerned
she felt deeply, and though she never showed how much
she thought of it, Edith's fearless love for Amy had wak-
ened in the mother's heart a new interest in the gentle
orphan. She silently resolved to show her gratitude by placing Edith in a happy home of her own, and for this reason
she gladly granted Amy's wish that Edith might be always
with her. Edith's natural grace and refinement fitted her
for any circle she might enter, and thus, though many wondered and some disapproved, Amy's lovely friend was with
her wherever she might go.

"You are here alone? Could Arthur find no one to dance
with you?" said Lady Ida as she passed along the balcony
and saw Edith sitting there.

"I have been dancing all the evening and am only waiting here for Amy," answered Edith, adding kindly, "Let
me offer you my seat, for you look pale and weary."

"Who have you been dancing with, pray, old Sir Harry
Lee or Doctor Morton?" said Lady Ida as she threw herself
into the seat from which Edith rose.

"Oh, no," said Edith gently. "Mr. Temple and Lord

Arlington were my partners twice, and I have just finished my third dance with Lord Percy. He left me here and went to find Amy, for we are going to the lake."

Lady Ida felt her proud heart swell with anger, for Lord Percy had not asked her once, and Lord Arlington had scarcely spoken to her since Edith came. With a scornful look, she said, "You are too forward, Miss Adelon, and should remember that they only ask you for Amy's sake. You should decline, for it is soon remarked when lowborn girls like you are taken notice of, and for your own sake I advise you to be more reserved and less bold."

"Lady Ida, what have I ever done that you should treat me so unkindly?" said Edith. Her low voice trembled, while the tears shone in her gentle eyes. "I am not bold and gladly would refuse them all, but they would not let me, and for Amy's sake I danced with them. If it was wrong, forgive it, and tell me how I can win your love. Why do you so dislike me? Have I in any way offended you?"

"Yes," said Lady Ida bitterly. "You are young and lovely, and in spite of poverty and humble birth, you win respect and admiration from those above you. You have no right to stand between me and my happiness as you do, and I hate you for it."

"I have no other home but this and no friends to take me in or, much as I love Amy, I would leave her and trouble you no more," said Edith sadly. "How one so poor and humble as myself can injure you I cannot tell, but if

it is so, do not hate me for the wrong I may have innocently done you, but tell me how I can escape it for the
future, and I gladly will obey you."

"Will you promise to avoid the guests who may be
staying with us and keep in your chamber as you used to
do before you rescued Amy at the crags? Will you refuse
to sing and take part in the gaieties about you? Will you
do this and by pleasing me repay in part the debt of gratitude you owe my aunt?"

"I will," said Edith, "if by granting this, your strange
request, I can win your friendship and goodwill. You cannot tell the happiness a gentle word can give me. Be more
kind and I will gladly promise to obey you."

"Thank you, Edith. It is only for a while, and I will
repay you for the favor you have granted." Lady Ida spoke
kindly, for her heart reproached her for depriving Edith of
the little happiness she possessed to gain her own selfish
wishes. They both stood silent for a moment, and neither
saw a tall figure glide quickly from a dark window just
beside them and enter a lighted one beyond.

"Amy does not come. I will go and seek her. Can we
pass through this way?" said Edith as she turned to enter
the small room beside her.

"No," said Lady Ida, "the door is locked. It can be
entered only from the balcony. Ah, here are Amy and her
party coming for you," she added as their gay voices drew
nearer and Lord Percy, Arthur, and young Arlington, with
Amy and her cousin Lady Mary Villiars, joined them.

"Are you ready, ladies, for a stroll in the park and a moonlight voyage? Stay a moment. I'll get Amy's guitar, and then we will be off," said Arthur gaily as he stepped into the small, unlighted room. A moment after, he returned, saying, "Who has lost a glove I found by the door? Someone has been romantically sitting in the dark. Oh, Percy, you've but one. Come now, confess."

"What have I to confess, save that I tried to pass into the hall that way and dropped it then, I think," replied Lord Percy, adding, as he took the glove, "Shall we not go? It is getting late and the moon is brightest now before setting."

"Where has Edith vanished to?" said Arthur as they stood on the broad steps of the terrace, looking down the lighted paths.

"I was promising myself a ramble in your enchanted park with Miss Adelon, but I turned to look and she was gone," said Lord Arlington.

"She is doubtless tired and has left us for a quiet hour by herself. She is not strong and often keeps to her chamber," said Lady Ida as she turned her eyes away, for she saw Lord Percy look earnestly at her and, conscious of the falsehood she was telling, it confused her, for she knew too well why Edith had so silently retired and given up her pleasure, as she had promised.

No more was said, and they went on beneath the lighted trees till the clear, cool lake lay sparkling before them. "Put our fair cargo in the boat and we'll lift anchor and away," said Arthur as he arranged the cushioned seats and handed them in.

"Lady Mary does not like to venture on the water. I will see her safely back," said Lord Percy, adding as he turned away, "Do not wait for me. Sail off. I will find my way to you again."

"A song would sound finely here. Can no one favor us?" said Lord Arlington as they floated on the lake.

"But for Mary's fears, Percy would be here, and he could sing divinely for us," replied Arthur. "I do not see him on the shore. How long he is detained."

"If Edith were but with us, we could spare Lord Percy longer," said Amy. "I am sorry that we did not send for her. She would enjoy it so much. Can we not row back and get her, Arthur?"

"No, no," said Lady Ida, "waste no more time but land us on the little island by the willow tree. Lord Arlington was saying yesterday how much he wished to see it, and it will look charmingly tonight."

"Hark!" cried Amy. "There is Edith's voice, but who can be singing with her? How beautifully they blend, dying so mournfully away, and see, here they come. Who is it standing in the boat?"

"Hush," said her brother, "do not call. It is too beautiful to end. Row into the shade, Robert, we will listen there." As they rested in the shadow, a small boat floated by, and in it stood Lord Percy, while before him on the cushioned seat sat Edith, her low, sweet voice mingling with the clear, deep music of his own as they sang a soft Italian air.

As the music ceased, they heard Lord Percy say, "I do not see them. Shall we not sail on and trust to find them at the island? As your boatman I wait your orders, Miss Adelon."

"Do I not see them there just in the shadow of that tree? Can we go a little nearer? I fear I am wearying you, but Lady Hamilton is anxious about Amy, and I could not come alone," said Edith.

"How can I feel weariness with moonlight such as this and music like your own? If the voyage of life were half as pleasant, few would wish it ended," he gently answered, adding gaily, "Arthur, is that you? Come out. You look suspicious hiding there."

"We are no pirates, Percy. Therefore, here we are," replied young Hamilton as their boat glided out and merry greetings were exchanged.

"Where did you find our missing Edith?" asked Amy. "We looked but could not see her."

"I met her seeking you, Lady Amy, with a message and a mantle from your mother. You were here, and what could I do but take the wandering lady in and follow?" said Lord Percy with a smile.

"Many thanks, dear Edith, for your care of me and the sweet music we have listened to. I shall ask to hear the song again, now I have learned how beautifully Lord Percy's voice accompanies yours. Row closer, Arthur, so that I can reach the shawl," said Amy.

As Edith leaned across the boat to speak to Amy, Lady Ida said, "Would you not rather sit with Amy? I will change if you would like it, Edith."

"Thank you. I am very happy here, and it might be dangerous to move," she answered, handing her the shawl.

Lady Ida took it rudely from her hand, and had not Lord Percy caught her dress, she would have fallen.

"Dear Edith! Are you hurt? How did you fall?" cried Amy as she saw her lean for a moment on his arm.

"I am safe, Amy. Do not be alarmed. A little wet, but that is all," she answered with a smile, though the tears were in her eyes at Lady Ida's unkind look and action.

"You had better hasten back, Edith, if you are wet," said Arthur. "James or Robert can row you, and Percy need not miss his sail."

"Thank you, Arthur, but I'm commander here and must see my vessel safely back," replied Lord Percy as he took an oar, "and I shall not miss my sail if Miss Adelon will sing. Finish your excursion to the island for Arlington's sake and do not disappoint your sister. Fair winds and a pleasant voyage." And, with a smile, he turned the little boat while the others landed by the willow tree.

"Miss Adelon, forgive my boldness and, believe me, it is from no idle curiosity that I ask if you are happy here," said Lord Percy as they floated slowly back. "I ask because

I have seen and heard unkind looks and words and could not rest till I had offered with a brother's frankness part of my own home to one who needs and so well deserves the tenderness and care of friends. Pardon me if I am venturing too far, but I have often sought for someone who would be a child and faithful friend to my aged mother. She is very lonely, for I am much away, and she would make a quiet, happy home for you and be a wise and loving friend. In the weeks I have known you, I have wished more fondly every day that she could have a gentle, pure-hearted faithful friend like you beside her and that you could be enjoying her quiet, happy home and that good mother's love and care. Forgive me if I have pained you, and let me serve you if I may." He spoke with gentle earnestness and a timid fear, lest he should say too much of what his kind heart felt.

Edith, while the bright tears lay upon her cheek, answered sadly, "I am deeply grateful for this kindness, and were it not for Amy and the love and gratitude I owe her, I would gladly be to your mother as a faithful, loving child; but while Amy needs me, I must stay, and for her sake gladly bear any little coldness or neglect and try to be more thankful for the home they gave me when I was friendless and alone. Again, I thank you for the generous offer you have made me and the kind thought that prompted it, and believe me, when I need a home and friends I will most gratefully accept the one you have given me."

"And will you let me call myself a friend and serve you as such?" he asked with a gentle smile.

"I am a poor and humble girl. You are Lord Percy. Then how can we be friends?" asked Edith, looking with her innocent eyes to him.

"You are poor and humble, Miss Adelon, but rich in woman's truest virtues and rendered noble by a warm and sinless heart. 'Lord Percy' is but a name and, casting that aside, I am one who finds his greatest happiness in simple things and cares little for the rank and riches of the world, for these are nothing to a noble human heart. Then can you not forget the difference of years and let me learn of one whose pure and self-denying life I reverence so deeply, and accept my friendship freely and as frankly as I offer it?"

"I will," she answered with a happy, trusting smile, and in simple, earnest words she thanked him for the kindness he had shown her. And when he left her in the hall with the hope that through his carelessness she would not suffer, she watched with tearful eyes till he was gone and then stole softly to her room to treasure up the gentle words he had spoken and pray that she might deserve so noble and so kind a friend. And in her dreams she was floating still beside him on the moonlit lake.

Chapter VII

In a poor and humble room sat Edith by a bed, where lay
a sick and suffering woman on whose pale and careworn
face a smile was resting as she listened to the low, sweet
voice beside her. When it ceased, she said, "Dear lady, read
no more. Pleasant as it is, it must be wearisome to you,
and you have still a long walk back. God bless you for the
comfort you have given, and think me not ungrateful if I
ask one favor more, but a mother's heart is ever fearing
danger for those it loves the best. Then may I ask you to
watch over my poor Louis? He is young and proud, and
in the home that Lady Hamilton has kindly given him there
are many things to tempt a gay and thoughtless boy. He
has avoided coming here and, when last I saw him, seemed
restless and unhappy. Then I feared all was not going well
but dared not ask the cause. You are near him and can
silently observe all that he does and save him perhaps from
harm and win the blessing of her who should be there to
guide and guard him. Dear Miss Adelon, forgive me if I
ask too much, but on my lonely bed I have pined to be

beside my fatherless child and longed most earnestly for some kind friend to whom I might confide my grief and who would grant my prayer and be a guardian to my poor boy. You are the truest one I have, and in you I have put my hope, knowing well the kind heart that can feel for suffering and sorrow."

"Nay, Theresa, do not weep so bitterly. Believe me, I will watch with all a sister's care over him and in my humble way do all I can to save him from temptation. He is a good, brave boy, and he loves you tenderly. He will, I hope, in all his troubles, ever turn to her who so patiently has borne her own deep sorrow. Do not fear for him, and rest assured a faithful friend shall be ever near him. Now let me bring some cooling drink and bathe your head, for you are feverish and weak."

As Edith bent so tenderly above the humble bed, Theresa's dim eyes rested fondly on the gentle form beside her, and she murmured softly, "He may well say 'tis an angel's face. None other could so tenderly look down on suffering and grief."

"Who are you speaking of, Theresa? Some new friend?" asked Edith as she laid a cooling bandage on the aching head.

"He told me not to mention it, but as he knows you, it can do no harm. I spoke of the kind gentleman who comes so often when you are gone. He reads the same book to me and speaks words of joy and comfort like your own. When I tell him all you have done to cheer my suffering life, he listens silently, while a smile so bright and beautiful shines on his handsome face. 'Who is he?' I have often asked, that I may bless him when I pray, but he always answers that your name alone is worthy to be whispered in my prayers. He stays with Lady Hamilton, but who he is, I cannot tell."

"Perhaps it is Lord Percy. Is he pale with gentle eyes and a low, sweet voice?" said Edith, while the color deepened in her cheek.

"Yes," replied Theresa, "but highborn and noble as he seems, few could be so gentle and so kind. And yet, dear Miss Adelon, no lord would come to my poor home and sit beside a dying woman with a face of such tender pity and speak such words of faith and consolation to a lonely heart. It cannot be Lord Percy, though the villagers can tell strange tales of all the good he does so silently."

"It must be he," said Edith. "And did you tell me he came every day?"

"The first time he came, you had just left me, and I sat beside the door, watching you along the narrow path and thinking how few young ladies would come that long, lonely way to cheer and comfort a poor thing like me, when he came round the rock that stands beside the spring and spoke so gently and said he was a friend of yours, that I told him all my story and blessed you for your care. He said little and seemed in haste to go. When he had gone, I found he had laid money on my chair. I watched him long, and he seemed to be following you as if to guard and yet not be seen himself. I loved him for his care of you, and in my prayers I bless this unknown friend and treasure his kind words with yours deep in my grateful heart."

"We will talk no more now, for you are pale and need some rest. Tell no one what you have told me, and prize the true and noble friend you have won," said Edith as she placed the pillows with a gentle hand and, with a few more words, she stole out. As she passed along the lonely path, she looked back often to see if her kind protector might be there, but no one could be seen, and with a new cause for gratitude and honor for one whom she already reverenced so deeply, Edith went her quiet way.

Theresa was a poor Frenchwoman who, in her younger days, had been a nurse to Amy and her brother and, as time went on, had won by her faithfulness and care the confidence of Lady Hamilton, who now, when she was ill and dying, gave her a quiet home and many comforts to repay her for the years of patient service she had given. She was a widow, and her only child, a boy of fifteen, was now placed by Lady Hamilton in her own home as a sort of page for Amy and herself. The handsome, lively boy was glad to show his gratitude by willingly performing all the slight tasks they might give him. But he was young and thoughtless, and in the pleasant home, now his, he daily learned of those about him to sigh for wealth and rank and soon grew discontented, sly, and sullen. His mother had soon seen the change and feared some evil might befall her child. She dared not take him from the dangerous home, which in mistaken kindness had been given him, and thus she had told her trouble to the gentle friend who often left the gaieties she might have joined to sit beside her humble couch and cheer the lonely mother lying there. Edith had promised to befriend the boy, and faithfully she kept her word.

As she passed along the balcony, young Hamilton came gaily toward her, saying, "We have been waiting for you, Edith. Neither Amy nor myself enjoy our rides when you are gone. The horses will be here by the time your hat is on. Amy is waiting for you in your room. Ah, Percy, you are just in time. I hope your solitary ramble has not wearied you too much to join us in a ride."

Edith raised her eyes as Arthur spoke and saw in Lord Percy's hand a little flower, which she well knew grew only by Theresa's cottage. The lonely walk was now explained, and when Lord Percy turned to greet her, he wondered why the gentle eyes were fixed so earnestly upon him.

"Is Edith going?" said Lady Ida as she joined them with her plumed hat in her hand. "I thought she never rode with us."

"She does when Amy begs her to, and I have a special message from her highness that Edith should join us, for it is too fine a day to paint or sing, is it not, Edith?" replied Arthur, turning to her with a smile.

She did not speak, but looked silently at Lady Ida as if asking leave, and when no answering sign was given, she answered gently, "Thank you, but I will not join you today. I can soon win Amy's consent and will enjoy the air and sunlight in the garden while you are gone."

Lord Percy watched the look and heard the low sigh that accompanied the reply and, turning to Lady Ida, said, "Will you not add your entreaties to mine, and we may win Miss Adelon's consent to go in spite of her refusal?"

"Oh, yes, if *you* desire it," she answered with a meaning smile.

"Where were my gallantry if I said no? Besides, it will just make up our number and none will have to ride alone," Lord Percy answered as he turned toward Edith.

"Go get your dress, child, and tell Amy to make haste," said Lady Ida, for his words reminded her that if Edith were not there, Arthur or Lord Arlington might join herself and Lord Percy, whom in her own mind she had fixed upon for her companion. She graciously consented, and when Edith and Amy joined them, she was talking gaily to Lord Percy, who listened silently, while playing with the little flower.

"Here are the horses and our other squire," said Arthur as the grooms and Lord Arlington appeared. "Now let us mount and be off. Are you going to try Selim again so soon, Ida?"

"No. I did not order him. How careless Robert is. It is too late to change now. What can we do? Edith, you might try him," said Lady Ida.

"I should hardly like to venture it. You would fear to ride him, would you not, Edith?" said Arthur kindly.

"Oh, no," she answered, laying her small hand gently on the proudly arched neck of the horse beside her. "Selim knows I trust to his good behavior and will not trouble me, I think."

"He were worse than a brute if he did," said Lord Arlington, who looked admiringly at her as she pushed the dark curls from her happy face, which looked so lovely in the shadow of the simple hat she wore.

"Lord Percy, I am waiting for you," said Lady Ida. "Let us be gone. It's growing late." Lord Percy helped her mount and turned to do the same for Edith, when Lord Arlington stepped by him, saying, "Nay, Percy, as Miss Adelon's squire, I claim this privilege and honor."

But Edith, placing her hand upon the saddle, sprang lightly up, saying as she turned her horse, "It can be no honor to aid *me*," and, with a bow of thanks for the help she had not accepted, she rode on and left Lord Arlington angry and disappointed at the failure of the little plan he had made to be her companion for the ride.

"She shall not be rid of me thus easily," he muttered. "Proud as she is, I'll win her yet." And he was soon beside her, watching with malicious pleasure while her color deepened and her dark eye fell as he whispered flattering words and looked the admiration that he felt.

"Do you see those clouds? Arthur, shall we not have a storm?" said Amy as she watched the sky fast growing dark with heavy clouds.

"Yes, we must seek some place of shelter. It will not

last long, and we are too far from home now to return," said Arthur. "Percy, we must try to reach that old barn yonder, for the storm is gathering fast."

They rode swiftly on till, as they reached a turn in the narrow path, a large rock rose beside them, which Edith's horse refused to pass. They tried to lead him, but he started back and obstinately stood where he first stopped.

"Use your whip, Edith," cried Lady Ida. "You are detaining us all."

"Kindness is a better way than fear," said Edith as she threw the whip upon the ground and, gently calling him by name, smoothed his shining neck and urged him forward. As if quieted by the kind voice, he moved slowly on and was just passing by the dreaded rock when Lady Ida, who was just behind, impatient at the long delay and rendered more so by the drops that now began to fall, touched the fiery creature with her whip, saying sharply, "Go more quickly, Edith. We shall all be wet."

With a spring, the high-spirited horse dashed forward and was out of sight before they saw her danger.

"Stay with your sister, Arthur. I will stop him," cried Lord Percy and darted off, followed by Lord Arlington.

"She is still safe," exclaimed the latter as they caught sight of Selim and Edith sitting firmly in the saddle. "How splendidly she rides. She is a fearless girl."

Lord Percy did not speak, but kept his eye on the slender form before him and rode rapidly along.

"For heaven's sake, look, Percy, the path ends there. She must be thrown into the water or leap that high wall. What shall we do?" said Lord Arlington.

"Stand still and trust to her courage," said Lord Percy as he checked his horse. "Our calling will but frighten him the more."

The horse rushed on, but Edith, with a firm hand, drew the rein and, with a leap, he passed the wall. "Now ride for your life, and God grant we find her safe upon the other side," cried Lord Percy. They reached the wall and, hastily dismounting, they sprang over, and there they found Edith pale but safe, leaning beside her horse, whose fright seemed banished by the leap, for he stood panting and gentle as a lamb.

"Thank God you are safe, Miss Adelon," said Lord Percy as he took the bridle from her hand. "Selim has proved unworthy of your confidence by this."

"It was not Selim's fault," said Edith gently, while the color rose to her white cheek as she remembered Lady Ida's thoughtless action. "He has saved my life and I am grateful. Let us now return. Poor Amy will be fearing I am hurt."

"Thoughtful for all but yourself," said Lord Percy. "Will you ride back, Arlington, and bring them hither? The barn we were seeking is just here. We'll join you there."

Lord Arlington obeyed, and Edith turned to mount her quiet horse, when Lord Percy said with surprise, "You surely will not leap the wall again, Miss Adelon?"

"There is no other way. I cannot climb over so encumbered with my habit," answered Edith.

"Then you shall pass through. This part of the wall is loosely built and lower than the other." And with a strong hand, he rolled the heavy stones away and led her through.

"How is poor Selim to return?" she asked, looking kindly back as she passed the narrow path.

"He must return the way he came," replied Lord Percy.

"Nay, do not try it. He may stumble. 'Twas a fearful leap," cried Edith earnestly.

"Surely I may venture where Miss Adelon has been?" he answered with a smile and, a moment after, just as the rest of the party hastened up, he leaped the wall. "Why, Percy, are you trying to outdo Edith?" said young Hamilton. "Have we not had danger enough? Poor Ida is still faint with fright."

"She had a cause for fear. I had none" was Lord Percy's calm reply as, with a glance from Edith to Lady Ida, he led the way to the little shed. Lady Ida knew well what he meant but, too proud to ask forgiveness for the danger she had caused, looked coldly at Edith, hoped she was not hurt, and then stood watching silently the heavy drops that fell around and pattered on the roof.

"Edith, the rain is falling on your hair. Come stand with us or put on your hat," said Amy as she saw her standing by herself where the rain fell through the slattened roof.

"The hat is lost, but I do not mind the drops," she answered, moving farther from the sheltered corner where they stood.

Lord Percy turned from the doorway where he leaned and saw the only place for her to take was by Lord Arlington and, with a smile, he stood beside her and held his hat above her head, saying, "Will you accept the only shelter I can give? The damp drops falling on your hair will chill you."

As she looked up to thank him, she saw blood upon his hand. "You have wounded yourself. How did it happen?" she asked.

"It is nothing but a scratch from the rough stones, and won in a good cause," he answered, smiling.

"But it was gained in moving them for me. It must be painful. Let me bind it with my handkerchief," she asked timidly.

"If you please, but 'tis not worth the trouble."

And as Edith stooped to place it on his hand, Amy saw a strange, bright smile rest upon his face as he looked upon her head, bent before him with the raindrops shining in her dark, disordered hair, which fell upon her shoulder.

"You can keep it as a love token, Percy," said Lord Arlington. "I should sincerely wish my arm were broken if I thought Miss Adelon would bind it up as carefully."

"Friends need no tokens to remember kind deeds by, and Miss Adelon has given me leave to number myself among her most sincere," replied Lord Percy as he saw her cheek grow crimson and the long lashes droop before the bold looks of Lord Arlington. "Do you see how finely it is clearing off? Our ride home will be delightful, as the rain is over. I'll go and see how our horses have fared."

"See what comes of gallantly turning your hat into a water bucket, Percy. You are as badly off now as Edith," said Arthur, laughing.

"Then we can sympathize in our misfortunes," replied Lord Percy gaily as she shook the water out and laid it down to dry, while he went to the tree where their horses had found shelter from the storm.

"Let us get home as quickly as we can," said Lady Ida, who had lost all pleasure in the ride.

"We need wait no longer, for here is our noble groom," said Arthur as Lord Percy led the horses to the door. "Why, Percy, you have changed the saddles. Who is to ride Selim home?"

"I," replied Lord Percy, "if Miss Adelon will trust herself on my well-trained horse. He is very gentle. Do you fear it?" he asked as she paused before mounting.

"No, it was but your kindness in thinking of it," answered Edith as she took the offered hand.

He gently seated her, saying, "You promised me the right to serve you if I could, and this is but a little thing to win your gratitude, Miss Adelon," and, with a kind smile, he placed the bridle rightly for her.

Mounting Selim, he would have ridden beside her had not Lady Ida, who had seen the grateful look in Edith's gentle eyes and heard Lord Percy lower his voice, now called him, saying, "I am waiting for my cavalier. Lord Arlington takes care of Edith and will follow us, for without her hat she is looking quite disheveled and forlorn."

"Then I fear I am hardly a more suitable companion, Lady Ida, for my wet hat has lost all shape and must be left to dry," replied Lord Percy as he rode slowly forward.

"You can place it on your saddle and none will know but 'tis from choice and not necessity," said Lady Ida, who determined not to yield. "Besides," she added with a scornful laugh, "you are not such a Madge Wildfire[1] as poor Edith is with her wet habit and disordered hair. I fear Lord Arlington will hardly like to act as escort to such a distracted-looking damsel."

"If all Madge Wildfires were as lovely as Miss Adelon, I'd gladly be her guard the wide world over," said Lord Arlington, who now rode close beside her. And as the fresh wind blew Edith's dark hair back, he looked at her pure, pale face and thought he had never seen a fairer one. As the memory of her courage, purity, and graceful beauty passed before him, he forgot that she was poor and humble and remembered only the selfish love he bore her. He lingered behind all the rest, stopped suddenly, and implored her to hear him and not to hastily reject the honor, wealth, and love he offered, but to let him hope that when she knew him better she would listen to his suit.

With blushing dignity, in few but simple words she thanked him for the honor he bestowed and kindly but decidedly refused his love. When he placed himself before her, passionately vowing she should remain till she had given another and a kinder answer, she repeated her refusal. Freeing her hand from his rude grasp, she touched her horse and, with a silent look of calm contempt, passed by and joined Amy and her brother, with the bright flush on her cheek and the indignant light still in her eye.

"Edith looking proud and Arlington angry; what can that forbode?" whispered Arthur to his sister as they rode through the park and saw how Edith urged her horse on, as if in haste to be alone, and how Lord Arlington rode close behind with a frown on his dark face and bitter smile upon his lips.

"I cannot tell, but he is bold and Edith is so pure and modest that such plainly shown admiration must displease her. Have you not seen her color when he looks so rudely at her? She never did before, though I have seen Lord Percy watch her long and often. Though she is poor, she is a woman and feels deeply when true courtesy and kindness are not shown her. Can you not speak to him, dear Arthur? I know she must dislike him and would be grateful to be freed from his admiration so disagreeably shown."

"No, Amy, I cannot speak to one so much older than myself and on such a subject. He will not stay much longer, and Edith can soon show by her manner if it is displeasing to her. I will do all I can to save her from annoyance, and Arlington will soon forget her in some other novelty."

And Edith, when dismounting, turned gladly from

Lord Arlington and took the hand that Arthur kindly offered and thanked him with a smile, which vanished as she met her rejected suitor's eyes fixed jealously upon her.

And now Edith had another trial to grieve and worry her, for Lord Arlington, to vent his anger and his disappointed passion, seemed to delight in doing all that lay in his power to make her feel the jealous love he still cherished for her. By looks and words, while seemingly most courteous and kind, he pained and wounded her most deeply. Still, for Amy's sake, she tried to be gay and happy, and though Lady Ida had not kept her word and was as cold and scornful as before, she steadfastly refused to join in all the gaiety about her. Her voice was never heard, save when she sang for Amy and when Lady Ida's silent consent had first been won. She gladly sought her quiet chamber and would have asked no greater happiness than to be free for a while from Lord Arlington's looks of love and Lady Ida's unkind words. But Amy, little dreaming of the pain her loving friend was suffering for her sake alone, would have her always near and wondered daily why Edith was so silent and why she stole away when all were gayest round her.

Arthur kindly strove to save her from all neglect and coldness but, as host of his hospitable home, he was seldom near her and knew little of the trials that she bore. Lord Percy silently looked on, and in each heart before him read a different tale: Lady Ida's pride and selfishness; Lord Arlington's ungenerous love; Amy's innocence and childlike joy; and her brother's frank good nature and his happy-hearted wish to make all gay around him. All these he saw, but the heart he studied the most earnestly and that each day grew more beautiful to him was Edith's. Amid the trials she so silently was bearing still grew the gratitude and love she bore to those around her and still lay the deep, longing wish for tenderness and true affection, which none ever guessed and none ever sought to give.

Yet he who was daily near her and who so often found a place within her thoughts now became her friend, seeking by unseen acts of silent kindness to make life more pleasant to her. While thus employed, the friendship and the generous pity were fast deepening into the truest reverence and most holy love for one who bore so meekly all the sorrows that must try a gentle heart and was so rich in pure and sinless feelings and so beautiful in all a woman's noblest gifts.

Chapter VIII

Edith sat reading in the pleasant garden, with flowers blooming round her and green leaves rustling overhead, when Louis, the young page, stood beside her, saying timidly, "Miss Adelon, there is a poor sick stranger at old Martha's cottage who needs help and care, and I made bold to come to you, for no one gives such aid and comfort to the sorrowful and suffering. He is old and looks like one who had known better days. I will gladly guide you if you will but go."

"I will," said Edith, and they soon were hastening toward the cottage where he lay.

"I told old Martha you would come," said Louis. "I will wait out here for you. New faces seem to trouble him, and he will see you best alone."

Edith entered, and the kind old dame told all she asked about the suffering stranger. "My husband found him lying by the roadside and brought the poor man home. He was suffering for rest and food but is much better now, though sadly weak, and some great sin or sorrow seems to haunt him night and day. He is grateful for the little we can do but seems impatient to be gone and finish something that he says must be performed ere he can die in peace. He is sitting up now. Come and see him, dear Miss Adelon; your words will surely comfort him." And speaking thus, she led the way into a small, neat room, where in an armchair sat a man whose pale and haggard face seemed marked with care and trouble more than age. He turned quickly as they entered and gazed earnestly upon Edith as she stood beside him, while old Martha said, "This is the kind young lady whom I told you of. She visits all the poor and suffering, and her kind, gentle words will cheer and comfort. I must go to my work, and you will talk best when alone."

"How can I serve you? Do not fear to tell me, for I most gladly will supply whatever you most need," said Edith gently as the old woman left them.

"Can you give me back my happiness and peace of mind and make me the honest man I was?" said the old man sadly. "No, no, you cannot give me this, and I need nothing else to save me from despair. Stay. Tell me what your name is," he cried suddenly in a hollow voice as Edith put aside the veil she wore.

"My name is Adelon," said Edith, smiling at his sudden question, but she started as he seized her dress, saying wildly, "Was that your father's name? Who were your parents? Tell me, I implore you. Are they living?"

"No," she answered, wondering at his strange request. "I have no parents. My father I have never known. My mother died long years ago in Italy."

"And were you born there? Nay, do not fear me," said the old man, seeing her shrink back as he bent eagerly to catch her answer. "You little know the fear and joy you have roused within me. Pardon my wild words and tell me, I entreat you, all you know about your home and parents, and let me, if I may, atone for my great sin."

Edith, startled by his trembling earnestness, sat down beside him and replied, "My father, as I told you, I have never known, and all I can remember of my childhood is that, with my mother, I dwelt in a poor and humble home with few joys but her love and no friends but a kind old peasant, who generously shared his little all with us and cheered my mother's dying hour by promising to love her orphan child, and faithfully he kept his word. My mother's gentle heart was broken by some sorrow that I never knew, and when I wept in bitter grief upon her grave and prayed to rest there with her, the kind friend to whose care she gave me cheered my childish sorrow. In his humble home calm, happy years went by till death left me all alone once more, and then I was placed with others in the orphans' home. There, in the tenth year of my life, a happy change took place. One day, while singing in the garden a sweet song that my mother taught me, a stranger heard it and, pitying my friendless lot, took the poor Italian child to his own lovely home in England, and there she has grown up and still cherishes a tender gratitude for all this kindness and the care that cheered her lonely life. That stranger was Lord Hamilton, and he died several years ago and with his last words blessed me for the little I could do to show my love and left me as a charge to be still cared for and protected. I have told you all. Now, answer me. Why did you ask so strange a question from one whom you never saw till now?"

The old man did not answer but, with folded hands, looked up to heaven, saying, while the tears streamed down his pale, thin cheek, "My master's brother; 'tis the hand of Providence in this. God has heard my prayer. Now I can die in peace.

"Ask me no more," he said as Edith looked in silent wonder on his joy. "I cannot tell the sinful tale with eyes so like your injured father's looking on me. Leave me now, for I must quit this place tonight, and ere long you shall know the great wrong I have done you and shall be repaid for years of poverty by wealth you little dream of now. Trust me, Miss Adelon; I am not the poor dying man I seem and with new strength will journey back to finish the hard task I had begun."

Edith feared his reason had been touched, for his pale face glowed and his sunken eyes flashed as he bid her go and, with a few kind words, she left him, wondering at the strange scene she had borne a part in and the wild words she had heard.

But they soon passed away and, in other, happier thoughts, she forgot the strange old man and his mysterious words. He left the village and was never seen there again.

Chapter IX

The rain fell heavily without, and Amy, with a party of young friends, sat in the pleasant drawing room trying to wile away the time with music and gay conversation.

"How can we get through the evening most agreeably?" said Arthur as he threw himself beside his sister. "It must go right merrily, for Arlington tells me he must leave tomorrow, and in honor of his departure we must have some new and striking amusement, as the weather forbids all outdoor pleasures. Come, Ida, give us an idea."

"Had we known it sooner, we might have prepared a little play. Do you remember how successful we were last winter? But it is too late for that now, and I cannot tell what would be most agreeable," said Lady Ida.

"That would make a fine tableau,"[2] said Lady Mary Villiars as she laid aside a picture she had been looking at.

"Let me see it," cried Amy, springing up. "It would be lovely. Let us have tableaux. That is new and very entertaining and needs but little preparation."

"We will," said Arthur, "for I see you all look quite inspired with the thing. So bring out the portfolios, and Ida, you must plan the dresses. Now, ladies, come and choose your characters, and we gentlemen will be kings or peasants, as you shall command." And, spreading out a fine collection of pictures and engravings, they all gathered round and were soon deep in their choice and arrangement of the various scenes before them.

"We must have this. It is so graceful and the dresses are so rich," said Arthur as he showed a beautiful engraving of Amy Robsart[3] weeping her farewell on Leicester's bosom. "Arlington would make a splendid earl, and who among you ladies can boast such long, dark locks as these falling in such fine confusion on poor Amy's shoulders?"

"Edith has most lovely hair, as you shall see," cried Amy as she suddenly drew out the comb, and Edith's dark hair fell in rich waves to her knee. "Nay, never blush and look indignant, for I shall not give you back the comb till you consent to be Lord Leicester's bride."

"No, Amy, do not ask me, for I shall not yield in this," said Edith, while her falling hair could not conceal the crimson blush upon her cheek.

"Then I shall keep you here until you do. No one will rescue you, I know, for they seldom have a chance to see such locks as these," said Amy gaily as she caught a long curl of her hair and held it fast. "Consent and win your freedom, or I shall keep you prisoner."

"Dear Amy, let me go. It is not kind to hold me here.

You do not know how hard a thing you ask," said Edith in a low tone.

The bright tears filled her eyes as she saw Lady Ida smile at her confusion and heard Lord Arlington encourage Amy not to yield, saying as he drew nearer, "Surely you will not refuse, Miss Adelon, to be a countess when a most devoted Leicester asks you?"

"I do refuse," said Edith as she fixed her dark eyes on his face, "for then, like poor Amy, I should find it hard to free myself so easily as now." With a sudden motion, she took a jeweled dagger from the table and, cutting the long lock Amy held her by, she passed quickly out, her glowing face veiled in her long hair.

"Quite a scene. Lord Arlington is pale with fright. Did you think she meant to stab you?" said Lady Ida, wondering why his eye had flashed so suddenly and why he watched Edith with a changing color.

"Oh, no," he answered, forcing a smile, "I had no fear of that, though these Italians are a fiery race. She was displeased with Lady Amy's little jest and at my boldness, I suppose, so we must lose this scene unless Percy will consent to take my part. What do you say, my lord?"

Lord Percy, who had looked silently on all that passed and well knew why Edith shrank from acting with Lord Arlington, now answered calmly, "Certainly not. Miss Adelon would choose to act it with none but a brother," adding, with a smile, "the handsome Leicester would feel little flattered were I to represent him."

"Well, we will have this instead. Rebecca[4] at the stake is as beautiful, and Edith would look finely if we can but win her pardon for our rudeness and the loss of this," said Arthur, lifting the dark curl Amy had thrown down as she hastened after Edith to ask forgiveness for her little sin.

"That is my prize, being won by my dagger," said Lord Arlington as he took the lock with a glance at Lord Percy, whose quiet kindness to Edith he had watched with a jealous eye and seen how gratefully she received it. "No one will dispute my right, I think," he added as he laid the shining ringlet by his side.

"I shall," said Amy, who now came smiling back. "Edith bid me take it, for she wanted no more trouble to be made about her nor her hair, and she has consented to act in any other where we cannot do without her, so I must deprive you of it, for if I break my word, she may refuse, and then our tableaux will be spoiled, for no one acts so beautifully as she."

Lord Arlington gave back the lock with a bitter smile, for he guessed why Edith had bid Amy keep it and, with a few careless words, he turned to the characters again and nothing more was said.

Evening came and Edith joined them, pale and calm as ever. The crimson curtain was let down before the recess where the tableaux were to be, and the gay party of young friends sat waiting in the darkened room till Arthur, as master of the ceremonies, announced, "Rebecca at the stake." In a blaze of light stood Edith, with the faggots by

her side and a heavy chain about her slender waist. A long
white robe fell to her feet, and her dark hair drooped about
her pale face, where a smile of joy and triumph seemed to
lie. With one white arm folded on her breast, she pointed
with the other to the unseen friend who came to rescue
her from death and fixed her bright eyes proudly on the
dark face of the Templar, whose rich eastern dress and glittering arms well became Lord Arlington.

"How beautiful!" cried Amy, who had stolen out to
be spectator till her turn should come. "But how strangely
proud and stately Edith looks. I thought she was too gentle
to look scornful, even in play."

"She feels it, and well she may," said Lord Percy in a
low tone, as if forgetful that he might be heard by Lady
Ida, who was just behind. She wondered at the words and
why he joined so heartily in their applause when the curtain fell.

The next was Mary Villiars as Queen Elizabeth, and
Arthur as young Raleigh spread his velvet cloak most
gracefully before her.

Again the curtain rose, and Joan of Arc, with snow
white banner in her hand, hair flung back and dark eyes
raised, stood pale and beautiful before them.

"That is charming. What a vast deal of expression in
the countenance and grace in her attitude," said Lady Arlington to Lord Percy, who leaned on her chair.

"Yes, Miss Adelon looks as I had imagined the heroic
maiden, fair and noble, with her brave heart beaming in

her face," he answered, as with a deeper color on his cheek he gazed, while a bright smile shone in his dark eyes. Another and another followed, some comic and some sad.

"Your turn now, Percy," whispered Arthur as the curtain fell. "The fair statue will be ready by the time your dress is on."

A few moments passed, and then Pygmalion and Galatea[5] were announced, and Lord Percy as the young Greek sculptor knelt before the statue he had made, asking the gods to give it life; and Edith, like a pure, pale image beautiful enough to be so worshiped, stood upon the pedestal, draped in a purple robe that glittered with embroidery, while jewels shone upon her graceful neck and sparkled in her hair. With a faint smile on her parted lips and a wondering joy in her soft eyes, she looked upon the kneeling figure at her feet, who watched, with silent happiness, his beautiful creation waking into life.

"How splendidly she looks and how well the rich Greek dress becomes her," said Arthur as they stood behind the curtain. "Percy's quite enchanted. Do you see how handsome and inspired he looks?"

"Who would not look inspired while worshiping so lovely a Galatea?" said Lord Arlington. "I should turn sculptor immediately if I thought the gods would bless my work as they have done Pygmalion's. Who would think she was the proud Rebecca who looked so scornfully on me?" he added in a lower tone, remembering the calm contempt he had seen in those dark eyes.

"Do not take your jewels off, dear Edith. We have but a few more pictures and then we are all going out to supper in costume," said Amy to her friend when Lord Percy led her from the alcove as the curtain fell for the third time on the blushing statue.

"We have been encored and are quite overcome with our applause," he said, gracefully removing the Greek cap from his head. Bowing playfully, he presented a bouquet someone had thrown them.

"How young and gay you look tonight," said Amy as she gazed wonderingly into his smiling, happy face, so different from the pale, sad one she had always seen before.

"Thanks to Lady Ida's tasteful skill, I think we all look younger and feel gayer in these graceful garments than in our own simpler dress," he answered. He looked at Edith, whose rich robe and brilliant jewels gave a stately grace to her slender figure and a deeper beauty to her lovely face.

The tableaux finished, the curtain was then fastened back and the young actors in their tasteful costumes joined their friends, receiving with gay jests and smiles the praises lavishly bestowed.

"Am I in time to claim the fair Galatea's hand for a waltz?" said Lord Arlington, bowing with much homage.

"I never waltz," was Edith's quiet answer.

"Your pupil, Lady Amy, does. Then why not join her? How can you sit when this delightful music is calling you away?" said he.

"Amy waltzes only with her brother. As I have none, my lord, you must pardon me if I refuse," said Edith.

"When will you grant me anything I ask, Miss Adelon? You would waltz, I think, if Percy asked you," said Lord Arlington jealously.

"He would not ask me," answered Edith with a smile.

"Too proud, perhaps, though he worshiped most devoutly well. The highest heads will bow to lovely statues."

"Lord Percy is not proud, for he has been a kind friend to me and many humbler even than myself, and is too sincere to show regard he does not feel," said Edith gratefully.

"Many thanks, Miss Adelon, for defending my sincerity. I will prove worthy of your good opinion by confessing I have heard what was not meant for me," said a voice, and Edith, starting, saw Lord Percy smiling just behind her.

"Pardon my offence, and tell me what you are pleading for so earnestly, Arlington."

"Will you persuade Miss Adelon to dance, Percy? I despair of getting a partner for this waltz. She has refused to honor me."

"I think the Greek maiden has done wisely, for a waltz would ill accord with the pure and simple manners of her native land and her own gentle nature," said Lord Percy with a playful smile. "But she will sing for us, I hope, and, as we have no lyre, a harp must take its place," he added. The waltzers stopped and someone asked for music.

Lady Ida, as she entered from the supper room in the

character of Cleopatra, paused suddenly and, with a flushed cheek and flashing eye, looked on the scene before her. Edith's graceful figure, with the jewels glittering on her white brow, stood beside the harp, looking beautiful and brilliant, while her rich voice sounded through the quiet room, where all stood listening silently. Lord Percy, in the Greek dress that well became his pale and chiseled features, stood beside her. Lady Ida, often as she looked, had never seen a smile of such quiet joy upon his face or such a tender light in his deep eyes as now, when looking on the bright form near the harp. He seemed lost in a pleasant dream and to have forgotten all around him.

She watched the look and smile, and in her jealous heart she vowed to win from Edith the heart she so unconsciously was winning and by false words darken the bright image she had made upon his mind. As Lady Ida passed among the happy groups, none could tell what bitter and revengeful thoughts were stirring in her bosom.

"Amy," said her brother as they sat together in a recess with Lord Percy, Lady Ida, Edith, and Lord Arlington, "did you know my friend Lord Hungerford had given his heart to beautiful Miss Grey, the pastor's daughter, and she has refused it? He is a noble fellow and loves her most devotedly. What reason could she have? Do you not think her wrong to refuse to make his happiness?"

"I did think so till Edith showed me how wisely she had acted," answered Amy.

"Why, Edith, would you, like Miss Grey, refuse a title,

fortune, and noble hand if it were offered you?" asked Arthur with a wondering smile.

"I should," said Edith gently.

"May I ask why?" said Lord Percy, who had listened with strange eagerness for her reply.

"Because poor and humble as I am, I should be ill-fitted to perform the duties of my high state. Miss Grey was wise in acting as she did, for Lord Hungerford, young and thoughtless as he was and blinded by his love, could not foresee the trials that would come when his humble bride should mingle with highborn friends. He could not know how bitter a grief would be his when he should see her whom he loved so fondly sneered at for her poverty and looked coldly on because of humble birth. She knew all this and nobly refused his hand, and by this seeming cruelty has saved his generous heart from sorrows that he cannot dream of now. To wed one so far beneath him in wealth and rank would be considered a stain upon his name and, with a woman's purest love, she has refused to win her own joy by the sacrifice of his hereafter. Is she not right, and will he not, when love's first disappointment shall be over, thank her truly and honor her more deeply for the wise, self-sacrificing friendship she has shown?"

Edith spoke earnestly and, as she ceased, Amy heard a heavy sigh behind her and saw Lord Percy's cheek was very pale. The happiness that had so changed him but a little while before had faded from his face, leaving it calm and gentle but so sad. As he turned away, none heard him murmur, "Again, the happy dream is broken, as it was long years ago. Would to heaven I were a peasant."

No more was said, and the gay party was soon broken up. "Good night, Miss Adelon, and pleasant dreams," said Lord Percy as they met in the hall.

"Are you ill, my lord? Shall I not speak to someone?" said Edith as she saw how changed his face had grown, though the kind smile still lingered there.

"Nay, I am not ill, but weary. Thank you for your care, but, after this gay evening, a little rest is all I need," he answered gently. As Edith passed down the long gallery, the smile faded slowly. He watched till the last fold of the purple robe was gone, and when he turned away, a single bright drop fell unseen. None ever knew how quietly that true heart's happiness had passed away, nor how the pure love treasured there grew stronger, though all hope was gone.

And Edith, in her quiet chamber, thought often of the gentle eyes that looked so long and earnestly in hers as, kneeling at her feet, Lord Percy saw that fair face smiling down upon him with such timid joy. In her happy thoughts, she had forgotten to take the jewels from her hair till, roused by the deep silence and the old clock striking one, she started up and, with them in her hand, stole softly through the dimly lighted gallery to place them in the cabinet that stood in Lady Hamilton's private room. As she approached, a faint light shone from beneath the door. "Amy must be here," thought she and gently turned the lock, when, to her surprise, the light was suddenly extinguished, and she saw a dark form glide behind the heavy curtain of the window.

"Ah, you cannot startle me, dear Amy; come out and show me how to place these jewels." And as she spoke, Edith playfully put aside the curtain but started back with a low cry of fear, for there stood not Amy, but the young page, Louis, his face deadly pale and his dark eyes looking fearfully at her.

"Louis, what are you doing here?" asked Edith gently as she recovered from her first alarm. "Do not fear to tell me. I will keep your secret, but I entreat you, for your mother's sake, do nothing wrong."

"I came to give a message to my lady," stammered the boy as he saw her clear eyes fixed upon him.

"Then why put out the light when I entered?" said she, adding kindly, "Do not speak untruly, but tell me proudly why you came. Stay. What is that before you?" pointing, as she spoke, to a piece of gold that he had dropped in his alarm.

He started, saw that he was discovered, and, falling on his knees, implored her not to betray him and he would tell her all. She promised, and he owned that he had taken money from Lady Hamilton's desk to purchase comforts for his mother, but he would restore it gladly and never sin again.

"My poor boy," said Edith kindly as she took the money from his trembling hand, "when next you need aid for her, freely come to me and all I have to give is yours, but do not take from your kind benefactress what she would so gladly give you. Now go, and rest assured that none shall ever know what has chanced here tonight."

With burning cheeks and downcast eyes, he thanked her gratefully and stole out with bitter shame and grief for his discovered sin.

Edith quietly went toward her chamber, glad that she had saved the widow's son from guilt and grieved to see how sadly he had changed. Suddenly, Lady Ida stood before her, saying sternly, while she cast a suspicious glance at Edith's pale and startled face, "Miss Adelon, why are you wandering here at this late hour, and what were you doing in my aunt's private room? I saw you come from there. You are alarmed at meeting me. What does it mean?"

"You came so suddenly upon me that I started, but not because I feared you, Lady Ida," said Edith, meeting calmly the stern eyes fixed upon her own. "I have been to replace the jewels that I wore. If you doubt it, you will find them in their places, and they are surely safe while Lady Ida keeps such good watch near them." And with a smile, she entered her own chamber and soon in happy dreams forgot all fear and trouble.

Chapter X

The dew was still upon the grass when Edith's light foot passed above it as she hastened through the park toward old Theresa's cottage. Four days had passed since she had seen her last, and she feared, from what her son had said when owning he had taken money for her sake, that she might be in need.

Edith's gentle heart reproached her for neglect. She had stolen an hour from the rest she needed to help and comfort one whose failing life she cheered and brightened by her tenderness and care.

"And do you really need no little comfort I can bring you? I feared you might be in want of something I could supply," she said when standing by Theresa's bedside.

"No, dear Miss Adelon. I have all my grateful heart can wish, and if I could but think my Louis was in a safer home, I should be content to close these eyes in peace forever, though why need I fear, when you are by him. I can wish no better guide."

"Does he ever bring you money when he comes,

Theresa?" asked Edith as she turned her eyes away lest they should tell the cruel secret that would break the mother's loving heart.

"No. He has no cause to bring it, for my kind mistress lets me want for nothing, and he must need the little that he earns to purchase the few pleasures that my poor boy has. Ah, if I were now as I once was, he should want for nothing that my toil could win. But why did you ask, Miss Adelon?"

"Do not look so fearful, dear Theresa. I will see that he shall be supplied in such a way that he will never know who sends it and will then be spared temptation and unhappiness. But I must leave you now and hasten back. I have promised to befriend him, and I will." With a cheering smile, she left the cottage and went quickly through the shaded path toward home, but suddenly she stopped, for just before her stood Lord Arlington.

He was soon beside her and, unmindful of the startled and displeased look that she cast on him, said rapidly, "Miss Adelon, today I leave you, but I could not go till I had pled my suit again, and now I ask you: Will you listen to my prayer, and in return for the riches, rank, and titled name I offer, will you give me but your heart? Once you have refused my hand. Again I tender it. Think well before you cast away what few would offer one so poor and friendless as yourself. Your grace and beauty captivated me, and I forget all else in the joy of winning you."

"My lord," said Edith calmly, "poor and humble as I

am, your wealth can never buy my love, nor your rank command respect for one who has rendered me unhappy by a selfish passion that cannot feel respect for my unfriended state, nor shame for the sorrow it has caused me, and that now seeks to win me by vain offers of wealth and honor that can never gain a woman's truest love. My lord, I thank you, but I have no heart to give."

Lord Arlington's dark cheek burned at Edith's calm rebuke, for he well knew how many trials he had caused her and how silently she had borne them all. Loving her the better for the patient strength she had shown, he passionately answered as she turned away, "To whom then have you given it? I know you seek to win Lord Percy's heart and must have gained it, or you could not cast by all I offer with such cool disdain. I have watched and now can read the secret of his kindness toward you, and I know you will gladly take the wealth and honor you now scorn from me when he shall offer it."

"My lord," said Edith, with a crimsoned cheek, "your words are false as they are ungenerous and unkind. Lord Percy asked my friendship and I gave it. More than this I cannot give to one so far above me. His wealth I do not covet. It never will be offered me, for he well knows I should refuse it, though not as I have yours, for he never would forget the kindness and respect he ever shows the poor and friendless, and he would never make his love a source of sorrow to one who never could return it. I have given you my answer. Now permit me to pass on alone."

"Never, till you have told my rival's name. You love another, or you could not cast me off this lightly, and I will not leave you till I know," cried Lord Arlington as he placed himself before her, pale with anger and looking darkly on her face, which never seemed more beautiful than now, when she was standing fearlessly before him.

With her calm, bright eyes fixed on him, she replied, "I have borne enough, Lord Arlington. Do not turn my indifference to contempt by this ungenerous resentment. I have given you my refusal frankly and with kindness. You have no right to question farther, and I shall not answer your uncourteous accusation. Let me pass. I will not be detained."

"I have guessed aright, then, and you love him, or you would deny it," said he with a bitter laugh. "I can read in your blushing cheek and downcast eye. I know your secret. He shall know it, too, and then see if you pass as coldly by when he shall plead his suit. Nay, never look so proudly. You shall learn to fear me if you will not love." With flashing eyes and lips white with passion, he watched her cheek grow pale with terror as she leaned trembling against a tree.

The green leaves rustled at her side and a clear voice cried, "Threats! For shame, Arlington. Stand back and let her pass." And, with a look of silent gratitude, she saw Lord Percy join them from the wood.

"I thought you were too honorable to play the spy,

my lord, and listen to a private interview like this," said Lord Arlington haughtily.

"I was looking for you when your loud voice drew me hither, wherein I heard enough to know Miss Adelon would need protection from your uncourteous words and most unmanly anger. I thought you were too generous to vent your disappointed hopes in unjust accusations and in idle threats, as vain as they were cruel. Be yourself, Arlington, and ask pardon for this passion."

"Your interference is as unwelcome as your words. Are you Miss Adelon's most rightful guardian, that you offer your protection ere it's called for?" was the scornful reply.

"Perhaps she does not wish it. Pardon my intrusion, and believe me, if I had known it was an appointed meeting and that she was left here by no force but her own will, I should have spared you my unwelcome presence and myself the pain of looking on a scene like this," said Lord Percy gently.

With a silent bow to Edith, he was going, when she turned to him, saying, while the bright blood mounted to her cheek, "It was no appointed meeting, and Lord Arlington can best tell whether I remained a willing listener to words that deeply wounded me and banished my respect for him. I am most grateful for your kindness and should wish for no protection save the presence of one whose friendship and whose honor I so fully trust. I fear nothing now and can go softly on." And without a look, she passed

Lord Arlington, and the winding path soon hid her from their sight.

"Forgive me, Arlington, if I have offended you," said Lord Percy gently. "I spoke warmly, but it grieved me to see you so forget yourself. You should have sought to win her tenderly. Jealousy and anger terrify and sadden one so pure and gentle as Miss Adelon. Can I do nothing now to aid or cheer you?"

Lord Arlington looked in the quiet face that smiled so kindly on him and felt the passion in his breast grow calm beneath the light of those sad, earnest eyes. But his love was still unconquered, and he said with a bitter sigh, "She has refused the wealth and rank I offered her and would not listen to me. Love, some other image, has a place within her heart. Whose is it, Percy? Tell me that."

"I cannot read the secrets of her heart, Arlington, but I trust whoever may be cherished there will prove worthy of the love of one so beautiful and sinless."

"She has allowed you to become her friend, and in return for this, shall you not ere long feel for her a warmer feeling and seek to call her by a tenderer name?" said Lord Arlington, glancing at the sad smile on Lord Percy's face.

"I should wrong the friendship she so frankly gave me if I could pain her by vain offers of a love she never could return and by rank and riches that cannot buy a noble woman's heart. No, Arlington, a true and faithful friend to serve and honor her I shall ever strive to be, but nothing dearer." In the changed voice and the heavy sigh, Lord

Arlington read the secret of the pure and deep affection that lay untold within that noble heart. With a self-reproach he never felt before, he stood beside the friend who had unconsciously taught him the beauty of a true, unselfish love.

They went slowly on along the path where Edith had just passed, both buried in their own thoughts and both longing silently to win the heart that neither could obtain. As they went through the park, Lord Percy stooped and lifted from the ground a handkerchief her name was on, and 'twas wet with tears. He laid it unseen in his breast, and none ever knew how tenderly 'twas cherished as the only relic of a love that never died.

"Where is Edith?" inquired Arthur as they gathered round the breakfast table. "She is seldom late. What has detained her, Amy?"

"I fear she is ill," replied his sister, "for I found her weeping bitterly in her own room, looking so pale and sad I could not bear to leave her when she bid me go and ask you to excuse her now. She will join us in the afternoon."

Lord Arlington looked up as Amy spoke and met Lord Percy's eyes, fixed on him with a sad, reproachful look. He felt deeply all the sorrow he had given and the tears his selfish passion caused her and knew well why she did not join them until he was gone. Amy tried in vain to cheer him, wondering at his silence and the sadness that so suddenly had come upon him.

At noon he left them and was waving his adieu to the

gay group on the balcony when he saw a pale face at a lonely window. His heart reproached him for the wrong he had done her and, with an earnest wish for her forgiveness, he bent low when passing and fancied, by the faint smile on her lips, that she had seen his kind farewell and understood it as 'twas given. But he did not hear the deep sigh of relief as the carriage passed from sight, nor could he know the quiet happiness now hers as this sad trial of her gentle heart was ended.

Chapter XI

Weeks had rolled away. Summer was deepening into autumn, and Lord Percy's visit would soon be over. As the time drew near, his cheek grew paler and the smile was seldom upon his lips.

Lady Ida fancied she could see the cause of this, for he was always near her and seemed to listen gladly when she spoke. Though he often looked at Edith, he now rarely spoke, and seemed, though kind and courteous as ever, to find more happiness away from her. Lady Ida sighed most tenderly and sang the songs he loved, leaning upon his arm with her most winning smiles while they wandered through the garden and the park, little thinking that her smiles were unseen and her songs unheard. When he walked so silently beside her, a fairer face was smiling on him in his thoughts, and another low voice sounded sweeter in his ear than the one talking gaily at his side. Yet in his calm, pale face, none could read the secret that lay hidden deep within and grew heavier to bear as, day by day, he saw those gentle eyes look gratefully upon him for

any act of silent kindness he might do. It would have light-
ened the burden of his untold love could he have known
how often thoughts of him stole into Edith's innocent heart
and how unconsciously her reverence and friendship were
growing stronger, though she never thought to call them
by another name. Arthur and gentle Mary Villiars were
now seldom parted, and Amy gaily joked them for the
long, lonely walks they took, while she, as happy and light-
hearted as the summer birds, knew nothing of the tender
secrets lying in the hearts around her.

"Edith, dear, put by this tiresome painting and come
out with me into the garden, where the sunlight and the
air will bring some color to this pale face. You sit here day
after day and paint as if to earn your bread. I will not let
you do so. You are getting ill," said Amy as she kissed her
cheek and urged her tenderly to come.

"Dear Amy, I am very happy here alone and am in
haste to finish this. Do not stay for me, love. I can see you
from the window and enjoy your happiness as if I were
beside you," said Edith. As she watched her young friend's
happy face, a bright smile shone upon her own. Turning
to her work, she forgot all save that by her patient labor,
she was gaining power to relieve the poverty and sorrow
that so grieved her gentle heart. If all the sketches her skillful hand produced were sold, she might then give happiness
to those who needed it around her.

At length she laid her pencil down and, as she pressed
her aching eyes, said half aloud, with a deep sigh, "Were

it not a sinful wish, I should long to close these weary eyes upon a world where I feel utterly alone." A few tears stole between the slender fingers and, as they fell, she did not see a kind face looking through the vine leaves clustered round the window or know the longing that one true heart felt to bless and make her life most beautiful.

A few moments passed, and as she resumed her drawing, Lord Percy entered, saying as he stood beside her, "May I wile away an idle moment here, Miss Adelon, and cheer your solitary labor with the poem that you wished to hear? It is very beautiful, and I should enjoy reading it if you will allow me."

The grateful smile that shone upon her face as she gave her glad consent showed well what happiness a kind word gave her, and as she listened to the low voice at her side, all weariness and sorrow were forgotten. With a bright glow on her cheek, she bent above her work as it went quickly on, while Lady Ida wandered through the park and looked in vain for her companion, who, with all sadness banished from his face, was sitting where he gladly would have stayed forever.

The poem was soon done, and Edith in her happiness forgot, as she conversed with simple earnestness, that she was telling all the high and noble thoughts that none ever had called forth before. Lord Percy, as he sat beside her, listened with a deeper reverence for the pure and tender heart she so unconsciously was showing.

"Miss Adelon, a stranger waits to see you in the hall,"

said Louis as he entered, looking with a wondering eye at Edith's companion.

"I will come. Pardon my leaving you, but I should not keep him waiting." And, with a happy smile, she passed out, little dreaming what awaited her.

The stranger was a countryman, who gave her a packet, saying, "An old man gave me this and, paying me well, charged me to bring it safely and give it into no hand but your own. I must not tell his name, and more than that I do not know."

After Edith thanked the man and rewarded him for his faithfulness, he rode away. She hastened to her chamber to examine the mysterious package, for the old man's strange words now came freshly to her mind, and, with a trembling hand, she opened it.

A few papers and a locket were all it contained, and her tears fell fast as she gazed on the picture of her mother and, placed plain beside it, the noble face of her unknown father, for her heart told her it could be none other. The first paper she unfolded was a letter from the old man, and this is the tale he told. While journeying in Italy, Lord Arthur Hamilton, the eldest brother of Edith's kind protector, saw and loved a fair Italian lady, poor, indeed, but of noble birth. They were married secretly, and none of his English friends had ever heard of it, for he well knew the poverty and religion of his gentle wife would win only dislike and contempt from his proud kindred. So he lived unknown in his fair Italian home, where a child was born to him, and, in the love of these two dear ones, he found a joy that never changed, till death took him away and left them desolate. While journeying from a distant city, whither he had been to visit friends, he was taken suddenly ill. Away from home, unknown and dying among strangers, he had no one in whom to trust except his servant, and to him he gave a casket in which he had placed his will and the locket he had worn about his neck, and bid the man bear it to his wife with his last blessing and to guard it faithfully till safe with her, for its contents were most precious. He died, and his lifeless body was sent back as he desired to the friends he had left. No tidings of his death were carried to the loving wife, for the faithless servant, tempted by the richness of the casket and believing from his master's words that it contained gold or jewels, kept it. When safe from all pursuit, he opened it, hoping to be well repaid for the sinful deed, but, to his rage and disappointment, he found nothing there but papers and a picture. In his reckless anger, he sold the casket, put by the papers, and then, fearing he should be discovered, left the country; and none ever knew where he had gone.

Meanwhile, the sorrow-stricken wife lived on, for she had secretly inquired and learned of the sudden death that had left her so alone. None knew of her marriage and none now would believe it, for he had died and left no will, nor any word to prove it true. Her friends would close their doors against her, and so, poor and brokenhearted, she toiled on for her child's sake, till, worn with care and cureless sorrow, she lay down and never rose again. She left the orphan to the care of a humble friend, who gave her a happy home till he too passed away, and then the friendless child found an asylum with others lonely as herself. Here she was seen by a noble stranger, who, struck with her childlike grace and beauty and touched with her desolate lot, pitied the little orphan and took her as his own, and, with his own fair daughter, she grew up to womanhood and never knew the secret of her birth.

Long years went by and, after leading a wild, sinful life, the servant of Lord Hamilton, while lying on a bed of sickness that he never thought to leave, repented of the evil deeds he had done and prayed for life, that he might atone for the deep wrong he had done his master's widow and her orphan child. He did not die, and, with penitent earnestness, sought far and wide for those he had so wronged. The wife was dead and the child in a distant land. There he searched, but all in vain. The stranger who had taken her was unknown, and the unhappy man was wandering over England in despair, when, worn with sorrow and remorse, he lay ill and friendless in a cottage. There came to him with gentle words the child he had so sinned against, now grown to womanhood, yet bearing in her face and name sure signs that she was daughter of the master whose dying trust he had betrayed. Her story proved his wild hopes true, and, with new strength and deepest joy, he hastened to restore the packet with a full confession, making the poor orphan girl the rightful heiress of her father's wealth. That repentant servant was the strange old man. That child was Edith.

With a heart filled with wonder, joy, and gratitude and eyes blinded by her falling tears, Edith looked with all a daughter's love upon the faces that seemed smiling tenderly upon her. Now, after years of loneliness and sorrow, she was proved their child. No more a friendless orphan, she now might claim the love and honor of her kindred and take her place among them as the fairest and most worthy of the rank and name now hers.

Long she sat in silent happiness, forgetful of the world around her, lost in loving memories of the past and bright dreams for the future, when suddenly a wild thought darted through her mind as she remembered that the fortune that she now might claim had passed to the younger brother of her father. That brother was the friend who had taken her, a friendless orphan, to his home and made her lonely life a pleasant one by his kind care and generous protection. As the bitter tears fell fast, she bowed her head and prayed for strength to do what her grateful heart had whispered was her duty.

Mournful thoughts of the loveless, solitary life now hers, of her poverty and her dependence on the bounty of the friends whose wealth was all now rightfully her own rose sadly up before her. The sweet visions she made of loving friends and kindred gathering round her when her strange tale should be known, of happiness and honor and the joy of blessing others as she herself had been blessed, all these fair hopes seemed brighter and more beautiful when now she must renounce them.

Long and hard was the struggle in that gentle heart, which cared little for wealth but longed so earnestly for love and kindness and so sadly felt the sorrow of a lonely life, but still strong and deep lay her fadeless gratitude. Silently she put away the bright dreams she had cherished and banished from her lonely bosom all the sweet hopes she had made of tenderness and joy. With the holy light of a noble, self-denying love shining upon her pure, pale face and in her earnest eyes, she placed the locket in her bosom, saying, as she kissed it fondly, "God forgive me if I sin in doing this, but surely it is easier to suffer poverty and sorrow than to bring such care and trouble to the home where, as a friendless child, I have dwelt so long and peacefully. I will destroy all tokens of the joy that might be mine. Though I put away this earthly wealth, I shall be forever rich in the peace of my own soul and the hope that these dear faces smile upon the child who strives to be more worthy of their love." Placing the papers in her desk, she hastened out to finish the great sacrifice she had begun.

As the door closed on her, a dark face appeared from behind the curtained bed, and a moment after, Louis, the young page, stole to the desk, saying as he opened the packet she had again refolded, "She has watched and followed me as if I were a thief. I will show her that I am no child to be so spied upon. I'll take the smallest of these precious papers and work some mischief with it and so be revenged for all her hateful watching." With these words, he hid a paper in his bosom, replaced the packet, and stole out with a dark smile on his face.

Since the night when Edith had discovered him with the stolen money in his hand, he had avoided her and seen with growing anger that she seemed to watch him silently. Forgetting all he and his mother owed her, he hated her for the quiet guard she seemed to keep upon his actions, and he waited only for an opportunity to vent his wounded pride and anger in some way that would annoy and trouble her. He had seen the stranger and had listened to the message he delivered with the packet and then had stolen to her room and there concealed himself to learn the secret that the old man had confided to her. By her tears and broken words, he had discovered that some great joy had befallen her and hoped by taking the paper he should destroy it.

Edith, little dreaming what had chanced while she was gone, returned bearing a light and, without another look, set fire to the packet and stood calmly watching while it slowly burned to ashes, and with it all the wealth and rank she might have won. As the last flame died away, she turned her sad eyes to the summer sky that smiled above her with a silent prayer that she might prove worthy of her parents' love and of the peace her sacrifice had won.

And with a heavy secret in her gentle heart, she left the chamber where so hard a struggle had been so nobly won.

Chapter XII

Days went on and Edith, with a deep joy in her heart, grew daily gayer and more lovely, for though none knew it but herself, she was surrounded by her family. They saw the color bloom upon her cheek and silent happiness beam in her eyes and wondered what had caused the change, but little dreamed they of the sacrifice the gentle girl had made for them.

"What are you looking at so earnestly, Lord Percy, and what fine discovery have you made?" said Amy gaily as she saw his eyes fixed on some object in the small boudoir adjoining the drawing room where they were sitting.

He started and replied, "I was very idly wondering why Miss Adelon should look so long and sadly at that portrait of your uncle. She has never seen him, I believe."

"Oh, no," said Amy, "we can none of us remember him. He died many years ago, but it is very strange what she can find in his picture to call forth the tears I can see standing in her eyes."

"It is because she can see the likeness that it bears to

our own father, Amy," said her brother gently, "and the memory of some kind word he has spoken brought those grateful tears, for she remembers with a daughter's love his care of her."

"It may be a foolish fancy of my own, but did you never think Miss Adelon bore a strong resemblance to that portrait, the same dark eyes beneath a high, white brow and a sweet smile on the lips? I have seen it often but never thought to speak of it till now," said Lord Percy.

"Yes," replied young Hamilton, "I can see it plainly as she is standing now. With that fine color in her cheeks, she does resemble him, but he was never married and her parents were Italians."

Little thought they while thus talking that Edith, with a daughter's love, looked fondly on her father's face and longed to call him by the dear name that her lips had never uttered, nor how hard she strove to still the tender thoughts that brought the bright tears to her eyes and made the secret of her heart so heavy to be borne.

"Mama, dear, you look sad. What has chanced to trouble?" said Amy some time after, as her mother entered with an anxious look upon her face.

"I am disturbed, my love, for I have lost some bank notes from my desk, and it grieves me to find that I cannot trust those around me," said Lady Hamilton as she sat beside her niece.

"Have you no suspicion who it was?" asked Lady Ida.

"For I have," she added in a lower voice, drawing her aunt's attention to Edith, whose cheek was crimson as she bent still lower to her work.

"As soon suspect my own child, Ida," whispered her aunt, adding aloud, "I know not whom to charge with it and fear to wrong some innocent person by my false suspicion. This is not the first time it has happened. Smaller sums have disappeared. You remember my telling you, Ida, of it some time ago. I took no notice of it then, hoping it would never chance again. I am disappointed, for a large sum has been taken, and now I shall not rest till I discover who has so deceived me, and whoever it may be, I shall instantly discharge without a character."

"Are you ill, Miss Adelon?" said Lady Ida, turning their attention to her changing color and the troubled look upon her face.

"No, I am only weary with my work and will go into the garden for a while," said Edith as she left them. She longed to be alone to calm the fear and sorrow that she felt at the guilt of Louis, whom she had hoped to save and whom she now believed had robbed his benefactress, thus adding sin to his ingratitude. Remembering the promise she had given to the mother, she silently resolved to beg him to confess by her entreaties and to win his pardon from the kind friend he had wronged.

"How strangely she behaves," said Lady Ida. "Did you see how pale and fearful she looked? She must know something of this matter. Do you remember, aunt, my telling you that I met her late one night coming from your room?"

"Yes, Ida, but she had been to replace the jewels as I desired her to, for they are very valuable."

"I think you told me about that time that you lost the first small sum," said her niece, who seemed very anxious to discover the thief. "I wonder," continued she, as if thinking aloud, "where she has procured the money she so freely gives away? Do you provide her with it, Arthur?"

"She has never asked me or I would most gladly give her all she could dispose of. But why do you ask such curious questions, Cousin Ida?" he replied, turning from Mary Villiars, over whose embroidery frame he had been leaning. "One would think," he added with a laugh, "that you suspected Edith of my mother's loss."

"And why not, Arthur? How can I help suspecting when I see so many things that lead me to believe them true? Nay, Amy, do not look so dreadfully indignant. I have not charged her with it, and for your sake will not tell my doubts."

"But hint at them, Cousin Ida, and I had far rather you spoke out frankly and told what you think, though all that you or anyone may say can never shake my faith in Edith's truth. I should as soon suspect you of an evil deed as one who is too pure and good to dream of ingratitude and sin like this," said Amy warmly.

And Lord Percy never thought her half so fair as now,

while she defended one whom he already loved and honored with a deeper faith than even hers, and he resolved to take no rest till Edith was proved innocent of Lady Ida's most ungenerous suspicion. "Should you recognize the notes again? If so, they might be traced," he said, turning to Lady Hamilton.

"I do not remember the various numbers, though most of them were small, I think, but on all of them I placed a private mark, thinking by this means I should discover them again."

"What was the mark?" asked Lady Ida eagerly, as an evil thought darted through her mind, and she turned from Lord Percy's glance to hide the sudden joy that glittered in her eyes.

"A small cross in the lower corner, where it would be least observed," replied her aunt.

"Amy, dear, lend me the key to your drawing box a moment," said Lady Ida, rising, with a strange glow on her cheek, adding as she turned to leave the room, "I am going to do what may seem a very dishonorable thing, but I cannot rest in peace while I fear I am wronging Edith by suspicions that I cannot banish. If innocent, she will readily forgive me. If not, I shall have served my aunt."

She left them wondering what her sudden purpose might be and waiting her return in silence. Some time passed, and then she slowly entered, looking pale and troubled, though her dark eyes gleamed with a look of triumph, which she strove in vain to hide. Lady Ida was a good actress, but she could not still the sinful joy and exultation that she felt so deeply in her jealous heart.

"How changed you are. Oh, what has happened, Ida?" cried Amy as her cousin looked sadly at her.

"Do you recognize this?" said Lady Ida as she placed a bank note before her aunt, with a dark smile on her lips.

"I do. The mark is here. Oh, Ida, where did you discover it?" said Lady Hamilton, looking anxiously into her niece's face.

"In Edith's desk," she answered as she raised her voice and fixed eyes upon Lord Percy's face. He started and the color vanished from his cheek, but he was silent and looked earnestly at Lady Hamilton, who sat as if bewildered with the evidence of Edith's guilt before her.

Amy hid her tears on her brother's shoulder, and gentle Mary Villiars tried to comfort her in vain.

"How did you find it, and why should you think it there, Ida?" asked young Hamilton, while his cheek grew pale with wondering sorrow at the sad discovery.

"I cannot tell what urged me on, but I could not rest till I was sure. Edith's sudden means of gaining money, which she never speaks of; her evident fear and confusion when the theft was spoken of; and my remembrance of her midnight wanderings to my aunt's private room and the notes that disappeared soon after, these things came suddenly before me; and while I feared to find them true, I felt it was my duty to save her from all further sin and my aunt from further loss. I knew the key of Amy's box would fit her desk, for she has used it when her own was lost. Thus I opened it, and in the secret drawer lay this marked note with several others and, grieved and angry as I feel at this deceit, I pity her and will do all I can to save her from exposure, if my aunt thinks best." Lady Ida spoke in a low, sad tone and placed her handkerchief before her tearless eyes.

"This is very dreadful," said Lady Hamilton at last, "to be so bitterly deceived in one whom we have loved and cherished from a child, one whom we thought so innocent and true. What is my duty in this case? I have said I would send out the guilty one without my pardon but, sinful as she is, I cannot treat our gentle Edith with severity like this."

"But will you let your love for her blind you to her fault, if she can repay your care with ingratitude like this? I think no punishment you can inflict too great. If she is pardoned now and should remain, our confidence in her is gone, and we shall still suspect and doubt her, and she will be unhappy here where her sin is so well known. Do you not agree with me, my lord," said Lady Ida, "that it is best for her to go?" She turned to Lord Percy with malicious pleasure in her eye at the pain she knew her words would give.

"I cannot doubt her yet," he answered calmly. "There is some mystery, which she doubtless will explain. Till then, it is a sin to blame even in our thoughts one who ever has been so self-denying and so true."

"I fear you would not be so merciful, my lord, were not the culprit young and pretty," said Lady Ida with a meaning smile.

"Were she the poorest servant in this household, I should fear to judge too harshly one whom youth and kind heart might have led astray," he answered, while his dark eyes shone. "Who among us, high and noble though we are, is so wise and sinless that we may judge the erring without mercy and the tenderest pity for the weakness we too might have had, had we been tempted in our poverty like them? I will not doubt till I must, and then I fear my faith in purity and truth will pass away forever."

"Thank you for this trust in one I love so well," cried Amy through her tears. "We will not deem her guilty till she shall be here to defend her innocence and prove how false all our suspicions are. Go seek her in the garden, Arthur. I cannot rest while such sad doubts of her are in our minds."

"She is not in the garden, Lady Amy, for I saw her leave the park not long ago, and by the basket in her hand, knew well that some kind deed of charity or love had called her forth," said Lord Percy, turning from the window where he had stood so long, and Lady Ida bit her lip in anger at this unconscious pose of silent watchfulness over Edith.

"We will not seek her now," said Arthur kindly. "Let her happiness, if she possess any, still be undisturbed till she returns, and then, when we are calmer, we will ask her to explain her seeming guilt. Come to your room, dear Amy. Your warm heart is well-nigh broken by this loss of confidence in one you love so well. Cousin Mary will come with us, and we soon will cheer you up." So saying, he led his weeping sister tenderly away. Lord Percy wandered on the balcony; Lady Hamilton retired to her chamber to gather strength for the task so hard to be performed; and Lady Ida, with the dark, exulting smile upon her face, sat in the lonely room, while bitter thoughts stirred in her proud, revengeful heart.

The long hours passed away, the sun went down, twilight gathered fast, and still Lord Percy paced the balcony and watched with longing eyes for the light form that did not come.

Amy and her brother joined Lady Ida and sadly spoke of the great sorrow Edith gave them. Lady Hamilton left her chamber with a calm, stern face and a firm resolve to do what she considered was her duty and, if Edith had so cruelly deceived her, to punish her ingratitude by banishment from the home that she no longer merited. Lady Ida, by every argument in her power, strengthened her aunt's intention and urged her to forget past kindness and treat Edith as she had deserved.

Twilight deepened into evening, and still Edith did not come. Amy wept in silence, her mother grew more anxious, and even Lady Ida feared some harm, while Arthur went to question the servants as to where she went. Lord Percy stole silently away to find her.

The lights shone brightly through the large and richly furnished room, and the night wind rustled softly in the crimson curtains as it floated by, bringing perfume from the sleeping flowers below. Lady Hamilton sat in her old, carved chair, while Amy, with the tears still in her gentle eyes, sat on the cushion at her feet. Lady Ida, with a troubled look upon her proud face, wandered restlessly from window to window and begged Arthur to follow his friend and find Edith. But he was listening to Mary Villiars' low, sweet voice and looking in her lovely face. Trusting all to Percy, he still sat where he was happiest.

At length Lord Percy entered, saying in reply to their eager questions, "I met Miss Adelon hastening home. She has been detained by sickness at the cottage where she was and will join you immediately. She is speaking a few words to Louis."

He turned to leave the room, when Lady Hamilton detained him, saying, "Do not go, my lord. I need your counsel and advice in this sad affair. Let me entreat you to remain."

"I will obey most gladly if I can serve you, madam, but I feared so many witnesses might grieve and trouble Miss Adelon," replied Lord Percy. Yielding to Lady Hamilton's repeated request, he stayed and, leaning on the high back of her chair, looked silently toward the door.

A light step sounded in the hall, and Edith entered. Her face was very pale, and some deep sorrow seemed to lie upon her heart, for traces of tears were on her cheek.

Still, no thoughts of shame or fear caused her clear, soft eyes to fall as she met the sad looks fixed upon her as she stood before Lady Hamilton, saying gently, "Pardon me if I have caused any uneasiness at my long absence. I could not reach home sooner."

"What has detained you, Edith, until this late hour? It is unseemly and improper for you to be wandering in the woods. Where have you been?" demanded Lady Hamilton sternly.

"By poor Theresa's dying bed," said Edith, while her meek eyes filled with tears at the coldness of her welcome home after the sad, painful task she had so silently performed.

"I trust I have not sinned past all forgiveness," she added gently as Amy kissed her cold hand tenderly and smiled upon her through her tears.

"Yes, Edith, you have sinned past my forgiveness, not for your kind deed tonight, but for a sadder thing than that," said Lady Hamilton, but her voice was milder, for gentler thoughts were stirring in her mind as she looked on the fair, pale face that seemed too beautiful and pure to hide a sinful heart.

Lady Ida whispered something in her ear, and she continued in a cold, reproachful tone. "You have forfeited my love, my confidence, and my protection, for, in return for years of warm affection and most watchful care, you have repaid me by deceit and great ingratitude. The missing money has been found. You best know where."

Edith's clear eyes did not fall, and no blush of shame tinged her pale cheek as she murmured, "Poor Louis, all is then discovered," adding earnestly aloud, "Believe me, I have tried to save you from the pain of knowing that your kindness had been undeserved and all your charitable care thus wasted. Deal mercifully with the erring and pity the youthful heart so sadly led astray."

"You do not understand me, Edith, or you are pleading strongly for yourself," said Lady Hamilton, wondering at her quiet sorrow, so unlike detected guilt. "The missing note has been discovered in your desk, and you are the sinful one."

"I!" cried Edith, starting, and she stood proudly up, while her pale cheek glowed and her dark eyes shone with indignant light. Her low voice trembled with emotion as she said, "And could you think this of me, could you for a moment doubt the reverence and love I feel for those who made the lonely orphan's life so beautiful by tenderness and care? Ah, Lady Hamilton, through all the long years I have loved and honored you, have I by word or thought deceived or wronged you? Have I not served you with all the constancy of a faithful, grateful heart, and will you now believe I could so sinfully forget the deep debt that I owe you and for stolen wealth barter the love that is the sunlight of my lonely life? I hoped you had learned to know and trust me far too well for this."

As the bright tears lay upon her cheek, she looked in

silent grief to Lady Hamilton, who would not show how deeply she was moved.

She answered coldly, "I do not wish to wrong you, Edith, but I must withhold my pardon till you can clearly and entirely explain how this note with my private mark upon it should be found in your own desk. Also the means by which you procure the money you have given so freely lately. By your evident confusion and abrupt departure when I spoke of my loss this afternoon, you roused our suspicion, and now, with this discovered note as proof of your sin, we must doubt you till you can convince us of your innocence."

"I never knew till now that I had enemies," said Edith sadly, "but that note I never saw, and who has tried to wrong and injure me by placing it there I cannot tell. Who first suspected me and who discovered the lost note?"

"It was Lady Ida," said Lord Percy quickly as he saw her pale cheek burn. She turned from Edith's calm eyes fixed upon her, and in that sudden blush he read shame at some unknown wrong, and in the pity of those soft eyes, the generous forgiveness silently bestowed.

"You ask me to account for the money I have lately given. I can do this and ask your pardon for what may not meet with your approval. I have sold the sketches you have seen me drawing, and some unknown friend has generously paid me far more than my poor work was worth. With the gold thus earned I have tried to cheer and gladden lonely homes and suffering hearts. If it was wrong, forgive me, but I could not ask of those who had already done so much for me."

"How are we to know the truth of this new tale? You cannot think we shall place confidence in what you say, Edith, after once deceiving us," said Lady Ida with a scornful glance.

"You, Lady Ida, least of all have cause to doubt my truth. A promise, when once given, is held most sacredly by me, even when others break their word and by reproaches make mine harder still to keep," said Edith.

Those proud eyes fell before her own, for Lady Ida well knew how faithfully she had obeyed her and resigned the happiness she might have, and what a cruel and ungenerous return her jealous hate had made the gentle girl. Lord Percy felt it deeper still.

"I can give no proof that what I say is true," said Edith as she turned to Lady Hamilton, "for the pictures are no longer mine. I know not who has purchased them, but could I place them here before you, with the price of each upon them, you would then see how cruelly you wrong me by doubts you never felt before."

"I place no weight on what you say, for no one but yourself has seen the pictures that you speak of, and few, I think, would pay so well for simple sketches like your own. You can give no reason for such unusual generosity. Therefore, I must set aside this tale of yours and still believe that money mine," said Lady Hamilton, believing from her own fears and Ida's hints more firmly than ever in Edith's guilt.

"This is very hard," said Edith with a bitter sigh. "I have lost your confidence and love, and no one will believe me, no one trust me now. Ah, if I but knew that unknown friend and could win back the pictures, that would prove my truth and I could suffer your suspicions with a lighter heart."

"They are here," said Lord Percy suddenly, and he placed a book before her, where lay all her delicate drawings carefully preserved. "It would be cruel if I kept my little secret longer, for here are full proofs that all Miss Adelon has said is true. Nay, do not thank me," he added kindly, as he saw the tears of grateful joy falling fast. "I but gave my portion to the poor through a fitter messenger than I could ever be and won for myself these tokens of a noble heart's unfailing charity and patient labor. Here, Lady Hamilton, are the sums received for each, and I now trust your suspicions are removed."

"They are, my lord. I should have known whose generous kindness had spared Edith from the difficulties her imprudent action might have caused, and I thank you for it; yet the first and greatest difficulty still remains, and I now ask you, Edith, as you value my protection and my love, answer truly. Did you take this money?"

"I did not, and God alone can know the bitter sorrow it has caused me" was Edith's firm reply.

"Then do you know or think who is the guilty one?

Do not fear to tell me. 'Tis the only way to win my pardon and lost confidence again," asked Lady Hamilton.

"Do not ask me this," cried Edith, "for I cannot answer truly and so must be still."

"Is this the obedience you have ever shown me, Edith?" said Lady Hamilton reproachfully. "I command you to reply. Do you wish to suffer for another's sin when it is in your power to prove your innocence? If you know, it is your duty to confess it and not shield the guilty one. Speak, Edith, and obey me."

"I cannot. I have promised. Do not add another sorrow to my burden by commanding me to betray the trust I have vowed to keep. I will work unceasingly till it be repaid. I will do anything but this. My word is given and I cannot break it, even though I suffer for the sin of which I am so guiltless," said Edith. She clasped her hands and lifted her pale face imploringly to Lady Hamilton.

"Then, Edith, I can no longer give a home to one who thinks a promise given to screen guilt more binding than the gratitude of years." Lady Hamilton answered sternly. "I shall grieve most bitterly for the unhappy fate you have brought upon yourself, but I can protect no one who thus repays my care with disobedience and ingratitude like this. I trust you may find happiness in some other home. Mine I can no longer offer you."

Edith bowed her head in bitter grief and still despair as she murmured, "Then I am friendless and an outcast."

"Not while Walter Percy has a home and a mother's love to offer you," said a low voice at her side. A hand fell softly on her lowered head and, with his pure love shining in his face, he stood beside her, saying, "Lady Hamilton, forgive this seeming disrespect, but I fear you judge too hastily. Some reason stronger than we know must thus control her. Give her time to think well of the choice she makes between you and her unknown friend. Do not cast her off. Remember all the faithful care, the grateful duty she has shown. Remember her youth and her friendless lot, and let the memory of your husband's dying charge render you merciful and tender to one who nobly suffers sorrow and desolation rather than betray the trust reposed in her. Grant but a day for quiet thought and rest, for she is worn and weary with the sad scene she has witnessed and may, when calmer, see an easier path to take and a surer way to win back your lost confidence and love."

"I yield, my lord," said Lady Hamilton, whose anger died while listening to his earnest pleading, and in a kinder tone she said, "Edith, till tomorrow evening I will give you to decide, and your final answer shall then guide my conduct. Think well of the choice you make. Your secret friend may be discovered and your sacrifice were then in vain. To keep my love or the promise you have rashly made, between these you decide. Now go, and at sunset we will meet again."

Edith turned to go, but Amy's warm heart could not be restrained, and as she kissed her fondly, whispered through her tears, "Dear Edith, grant our prayer and do not leave us. I shall lose my sister and my friend when you are gone. Oh, do as we desire and all will then be well."

"I cannot, dearest Amy. Do not ask me, for you cannot know the promise I have given." Without another word, she left them.

In her silent chamber, mid the bitter tears that fell, came the memory of the kind hand falling softly on her lonely head, as if to guard her when most friendless and forsaken, and the low voice pleading tenderly for her when others doubted and condemned. And in her sorrowing heart, a deep joy came like sunlight shining on the dark cloud of her grief and made all brightness even there.

Beside Theresa in her last hour, she had renewed her promise to befriend the boy, now left an orphan like herself. That vow to the dying mother was too sacred to be broken. She silently resolved to save poor Louis from disgrace and danger by refusing to confess what she alone could tell, hoping she might be allowed to repay all that had been taken and in secret might lead back the erring boy to duty and to happiness again, for she well knew his proud heart would soon break should his disgrace be known. This she had resolved while hastening from the cottage through the lonely woods. But when the note was found, and all the sin was charged to her, and Lady Hamilton disowned and cast her off, she still, through all her sorrow and despair, was faithful to her promise, and through the sleepless night her purpose but grew stronger, and she waited calmly what should come.

Chapter XIII

Sad were the faces and heavy were the hearts that gathered in the pleasant room when morning came. Amy's bright eyes filled with tears as she looked silently at Edith's empty chair and longed to be beside her to comfort and to cheer. But Lady Hamilton had forbidden it, and Amy dared not disobey.

Nothing was said of Edith or the cause of her absence, though Amy saw Lord Percy look sadly at the deserted corner where Edith's paintings lay, as if he missed the gentle face he loved to watch so silently. Lady Ida was the only one who smiled, and though she strove to be as gay as ever, something seemed to weigh her spirits down. A restless, anxious look was on her face, as if some trial was at hand which she longed for and yet feared.

As they were sitting silently together before they separated to their different pleasant occupations, Louis, the young page who had been absent since the night before, suddenly entered. His face was pale and haggard, but a strange fire shone in his dark eyes as he stood before his mistress, saying in a voice he tried in vain to render firm, "I have come from my mother's deathbed to confess my sin and save my truest friend from the shame she is suffering for me. Miss Adelon is innocent, my lady, for 'twas I who robbed you." The poor boy hid his face in his hands and could say no more. They sat in silent wonder at this sudden discovery.

No one spoke till Lady Hamilton asked kindly, for she pitied his distress, "What could have tempted you, Louis, to wrong me thus and let another bear your guilt? Do not weep so bitterly, but tell me all. I will forgive you for your mother's sake."

"Thank heaven she can never know how sinful I am grown," sighed Louis as he dashed his tears away. With his eyes bent on the ground, he said, "I will confess it all, my lady; she shall bear no more for me. When you first kindly gave me your protection and a home, I was as innocent as a child, but as I mingled with the servants round me, I was led astray. Young and thoughtless, I forgot the sorrow and remorse I should soon bring upon myself. I learned to gamble, and all that I possessed soon went. I owed them more. They threatened to betray me. I knew 'twould break my mother's heart and, too proud to beg, I was weak enough to steal. I went at night to where I knew your gold was kept. I took a little and was replacing the rest when Miss Adelon discovered me, and I confessed it all. She gently rebuked me for my ingratitude to you and bid me come to her when I was poor. I promised to obey her, but I dared not tell her all nor ask for the large sum I owed. They had me in their power. I feared disgrace more than sin, and I stole again. It was not discovered and, grown bolder, I took smaller sums and sank still deeper into trouble and distress. They tempted me again to gamble, and I soon lost all I had so sinfully obtained. At last, in my despair, I stole the notes and freed myself from them forever and made a vow to sin no more. Miss Adelon suspected me and watched. I was proud and willful, and I hated her for knowing how ungrateful I had grown and, to revenge myself, I stole a paper I had seen her shed tears over and heard her call most precious. I took it, little knowing that she was the unknown friend who sent me gifts and tried to save me. But all this I learned last night. My mother, on her dying bed, told me how, like a loving sister, she had watched above me and by silent care and unseen acts of kindness tried to keep me from temptation and from sin and had promised to befriend me, through grief or joy, till I should need her care no longer. And my mother's last words were a blessing on the friend who had cheered her lonely life with tenderness and love. Then in my heart I silently resolved to tell you all and by my own confession save Miss Adelon from further sorrow. I have kept my word. You know all now. Oh, my lady, pity and forgive me." Overcome with shame and grief, he knelt before Lady Hamilton and wept bitterly.

"My poor boy, I do forgive you, led astray by others whom you trusted. 'Tis an easy thing to sin. Your youth and your repentance have won my pardon for what might have caused great pain and sorrow. But now, tell me, Louis, how you discovered that Miss Adelon had been suspected of your theft. I have told no one save these present. How then did you know we doubted her integrity and truth?"

"Had I not so deeply injured her already, I could not answer this, my lady, but I must to prove her innocence, though it will grieve and trouble you," said Louis as he rose and fixed his dark eyes full on Lady Ida's face, which suddenly grew pale, while a deadly fear shot through her heart.

"When they told me yesterday that my mother was so ill," continued the boy, "I hastened to find Miss Adelon, knowing that no one could cheer and comfort her last hours so well. As I approached her room, I saw Lady Ida, with a strange smile on her face, enter it. I stole silently along and, looking through the half-closed door, saw her open the desk and examine all that was there. At last, she took a bank note from the drawer and made some mark upon it, saying as she did so, 'This will ruin her, and then I shall be freed from one I hate.' "

"It's false," cried Lady Ida, who had sat as if spellbound to her seat. "How dare you charge me with a deed like that!" She turned her flashing eyes upon the boy.

Louis, looking proudly in her face, replied, "It is true, and here is the paper where you tried the mark before you placed it on the note. It is a little cross. I took it from the table when you had gone."

He laid the paper before Lady Hamilton, who said sternly, while her face grew deathly pale, "These words are your writing, Ida, and the mark the same upon the note. Why have you done this shameful deed to injure one who never harmed you?"

"Because I hated her," cried Lady Ida wildly as she rushed from the room.

"Edith is innocent. Thank heaven for that," said Amy when the first moment of wondering sorrow passed.

"Yes, Amy, and shall be nobly rewarded for all she has suffered by our warmest reunion and love. You are forgiven, Louis. You may go," said Lady Hamilton sadly, for her niece's most dishonorable action had deeply wounded her.

"I have not told all yet, my lady," said the boy. "The paper that I took I have not yet returned. A strange old man sent her a packet with this and another paper and a locket, which she kept. She burned the other letters and doubtless thinks she has destroyed this, too. Will you restore it to her and win my pardon for the sorrow I have caused one who has done so much for me?" Laying the paper on the table by her side, he bowed and left them.

Lady Hamilton opened the paper, read a few lines, and then, pale and trembling, sank back in her chair, saying faintly, "Arthur, 'tis your uncle's will, and Edith is his child."

They gathered round her, and young Hamilton read aloud the paper that proved Edith to be their cousin and the rightful heiress of the wealth they now possessed.

"God has ordered it all for the best," said Lady Hamilton as he ceased. "We now must depend on her and trust to the love she bears us."

"Why should she burn what brings her rank and wealth? What can it mean?" said Arthur, wondering at the strange tale they had heard from Louis.

"She knew that if she claimed it, you were poor, and she would silently destroy all proof of her high birth, and with a noble woman's truest love, has chosen poverty and the wealth of a sinless heart and put aside all earthly riches, showing us the holiest gratitude and how deeply we have wronged her." And, as he ceased, Lord Percy turned away to hide the strong emotion that this sacrifice of her he had loved and reverenced so long and silently had caused.

"What ought we to do, my son?" asked Lady Hamilton.

"There is but one honorable way, and that way I shall take. Ask of Edith all she knows of this mysterious discovery, and then give her back her father's wealth and with it all the love, the reverence and honor that we feel for one whose noble sacrifice has taught us such a lesson of gratitude and truth," said Arthur. His fine face glowed with the feelings stirring in his noble heart.

"Let me go to Edith and ask pardon for the sorrow

and neglect she has suffered. She is bound more closely to us than before but never can be dearer to our hearts than now," cried Amy, as she longed to tell her overflowing love and weep her gratitude on Edith's gentle bosom.

"No, my love, not now. We must all wait till we are calmer ere we meet one who is mistress here. Go rather to your cousin Ida and tell her who our friendless Edith has become and whom she has so hated and so wronged," replied Lady Hamilton. Turning to her son as Amy hastened away, she said, "Do not seek Edith till she joins us at sunset, and meanwhile, as Lord Percy has gone silently away, come with me to my room, for we have much to talk of and I need your help and counsel."

Chapter XIV

Sunset came, and all save Lady Ida assembled in the drawing room and, heedless of the lovely scene without, sat waiting with far different feelings than they had expected. The evening light shone softly in and lit up Edith's fair, pale face, which looked so calm and sad in the rosy glow that fell upon it as she stood at length before them.

"We wait for your decision, Edith," said Lady Hamilton. Her voice was strangely kind and tender as she looked upon the slender form drooping before her, wondering at the strong, true heart that beat within.

"Forgive me that I grieve you thus, but I am still unchanged. The promise given I cannot break. Do with me as you will, but, ah, remember when I am gone that even when suspected and deserted most, I still was true and grateful to the last."

Lady Hamilton controlled the tears that rose, saying as she laid the will before her, "We know all, Edith, and here give you back the wealth that you so generously put by.

Louis has confessed his sin and that he took this paper from the others that you burned. He has restored it, and now take again all you have lost, and with it our truest love and gratitude for the sacrifice you have so nobly made. You are the rightful mistress here and will use well the power you have won."

"This is the first and last use I shall ever make of it," said Edith. She tore the will and, with a calm smile on her pale face and a holy light in her soft eyes that shone through falling tears, she dropped the fragments, saying, "Now I am the poor orphan girl again. Can you love me for myself alone and forget that I have any right to the rank and wealth that are so worthless to one who only longs for tenderness and love? I had fondly hoped this never would be known and I might hide the secret in my grateful heart and love you as my kindred, though I might never call you by the dear names that I longed to speak, and prayed that by this silent deed I might become more worthy of the kindness and protection you had shown the friendless child. This cannot be, but now take all that I can give, and in return for this act, let me call you mother and be a faithful, loving child, for you can never know how sad it is to be so young and yet so utterly alone."

And as her own tears fell, proud Lady Hamilton folded Edith to her heart and blessed her for her grateful love. The evening sunlight stealing in lit up those happy faces and cast golden shadows on the gentle head that bowed in silent thankfulness for all the love and joy that pure, young heart had won.

Lady Ida sat alone with a heavy heart. She had learned all, and Edith, whom she had so hated and so deeply wronged, was heiress of the wealth and honor she had so often coveted. Young, beautiful, and rich—how fair a future was before her. And as she thought this, bitter tears flowed down her cheek, and her own lot seemed darker and more dreary still. Poor and growing daily more unlovely, her proud spirit was humbled and disgraced by her discovered sin. Lord Percy's love and the respect of those around her were now forever lost. Bowed with sorrow, despair, and disappointed hopes, she wept burning tears of self-reproach and shame.

Soft arms were thrown around her, and a low voice whispered tenderly, "Dear Lady Ida, let me comfort you. The past is all forgotten and forgiven. We are cousins. Now let us be friends." And Edith's sweet face bent down.

Chapter XV

A long night and a happy day had passed. All had been told, and Edith, with her fair face radiant with joy, wandered through the home now hers, and all about her seemed a blissful dream. Loving faces smiled upon her, dear voices whispered tender words, and kind hands pressed her own. But still, amid all her happiness, one face came oftenest to her heart, and with it tender memories and sweet thoughts. When she saw Lord Percy sit so pale and still among them, she longed earnestly to share her happiness with him and cheer his sorrow. She little dreamed of the hard struggle between his love and the fear lest he should grieve if he told it, nor how he stilled the pleadings of his heart and silently resolved he would not cause another sorrow to one who had so patiently borne many by offering a love he feared she never could return.

"How often we have stood here looking on this scene, but never has it seemed so beautiful as now, when with Cousin Edith by my side I can look on it and feel it is her own," said Arthur fondly as they sat again upon the balcony, while the summer sky was bright with evening clouds.

"I fear it is the last time I shall see it for a long while, Arthur, for tomorrow I must say farewell," said Lord Percy as he looked at Edith with a silent blessing in his heart.

"You must not go," cried Amy. "We shall be so sad and lonely here without you. Shall we not, dear Edith?"

"Yes" was the low reply. The happy smile that Arthur's kind words had brought faded from Edith's face. Lord Percy heard a deep sigh as she turned and walked away, and he saw a bright tear fall.

When Edith reached the quiet seat beneath the old tree, she bowed her face upon her hands and felt how deeply she had learned to love him and how joyless life would seem when he was gone, for he had forgotten poverty and humble birth to be a true and faithful friend when others most neglected her. By gentle words and silent acts of kindness, he had won her reverence and trust, which now had deepened into woman's truest, purest love. "Of all my friends, I shall have lost the dearest and the best when he is gone," she murmured sadly.

"Lady Edith," said a low voice near her, and she started, for he stood before her with all his untold love shining in the earnest eyes that looked so tenderly upon her. "Forgive me that I dared to follow you, but my heart bid me come, and I am here to ask you if the love I have cherished long and silently can be returned. I never thought to tell it, but the sorrow my departure caused you woke a new hope in my heart, and I could silence it no longer. Do not think your newfound wealth and rank have tempted me, for God knows I would most joyfully have won you when most poor and friendless, for I had learned the priceless worth of a pure heart, rich in woman's truest virtues and most holy faith. But you had said you could not give your hand to one above you in rank and wealth, and from that hour my love was hopeless, but it never died. Each day some new deed of tenderness and care, some gentle look or word of yours made it stronger and more heavy to be borne. We now are equals in mere worldly riches. Can you give your heart to one who so ill deserves the blessing you bestow and trust me with the precious gift that shall be held most sacred until death?"

"I can." And, with her tearful eyes turned trustingly to him, Edith laid her hand in his and pledged her love. "I can bring you nothing but a grateful heart, whose constancy and deep affection can never pass away. Take me poor and erring as I am, and teach me to be worthy of the great happiness I have won."

"Oh, Edith," said Lord Percy. His fond eyes rested tenderly upon the head bent down before him. "I need no richer dowry than the love of such a heart. And though I take you without earthly wealth, still in the tender reverence and fadeless gratitude of those you bless, surely, dearest, you have won a nobler Inheritance."

EXPLANATORY NOTES

1. *Madge Wildfire*: A crazed character in *The Heart of Midlothian* (1818) who is done in by a mob. This is one of the three novels by Sir Walter Scott (1771–1832) directly referred to in *The Inheritance*.

2. *tableau*: A tableau vivant is a staged scene presented by people in character who do not speak or move during the performance.

3. *Amy Robsart*: In Scott's *Kenilworth* (1821), Amy Robsart is married to Robert Dudley, the Earl of Leicester. Because he fears for his position at court, Leicester keeps his marriage a secret, leading to a series of intrigues that result in Amy's death.

4. *Rebecca*: A character in Scott's *Ivanhoe* (1819), she is abducted by the Templar knight Sir Brian de Bois-Guilbert and is saved from being burned at the stake by Wilfred of Ivanhoe.

5. *Pygmalion and Galatea*: In Greek legend, Pygmalion fell in love with a statue and, at his request, it was given life as Galatea by the goddess Aphrodite.